THE SECRET SOCIETY OF VERY IMPORTANT POST

THE SECRET SOCIETY OF VERY IMPORTANT POST

ALEXANDRA PAGE

ILLUSTRATED BY

Penny Neville-Lee

BLOOMSBURY
CHILDREN'S BOOKS
LONDON OXFORD NEW YORK NEW DELHI SYDNEY

BLOOMSBURY CHILDREN'S BOOKS
Bloomsbury Publishing Plc
50 Bedford Square, London WC1B 3DP, UK
29 Earlsfort Terrace, Dublin 2, Ireland

BLOOMSBURY, BLOOMSBURY CHILDREN'S BOOKS and the Diana logo are
trademarks of Bloomsbury Publishing Plc

First published in Great Britain in 2024 by Bloomsbury Publishing Plc

A catalogue record for this book is available from the British Library

ISBN: PB: 978-1-5266-4433-6; eBook: 978-1-5266-4430-5; ePDF: 978-1-526-64432-9

2 4 6 8 10 9 7 5 3 1

Typeset by RefineCatch Limited, Bungay, Suffolk
Printed and bound in Great Britain by CPI Group (UK) Ltd, Croydon CR0 4YY

To find out more about our authors and books visit www.bloomsbury.com
and sign up for our newsletters

For my wonderful dad, Julian

AP

For Oren & Robin

PNL

1

Postage and Packing

Penny packed her letters last.

From beneath her bed she slid out a shoebox and blew the dust off the lid. Then, pulling her coat a little tighter around her for warmth, she perched on the edge of her bare mattress and opened it. Inside was a neatly sorted pile of leaf-like envelopes tied up with string. Each one was folded from a scrap of parcel paper and about a quarter of the size of an ordinary letter, because these letters were anything but ordinary.

Penny chose the top envelope from the pile,

unfolded the miniature letter inside and read it once more. Her mouth tugged into a smile as the tiny, wobbly handwriting played Wishyouwas's voice back to her like a gramophone record:

30th April 1953

Dear Penny

I hope you is good?

The Lost Letter Bureau is very busy. Thiswayup gived me something for you. I is hoping to come and see you soon. We all misses you.

Forever yours,

WISHYOUWAS

Penny glanced again at the date on the letter and her cheeks flushed with guilt. Even though Wishyouwas belonged to a secretive society of creatures unknown to most humans, the springy, furry little Sorter was her friend. Ever since Penny saved Wishyouwas from a rat trap at her uncle's post office last Christmas, they had trusted each other and told each other everything. At least, they had until now. This letter had been sent over a month ago, and Penny still hadn't written back. Not since Mum told her the really big news that had changed everything.

Penny had tried to reply to Wishyouwas but somehow she couldn't find the right words to tell him. And the longer she waited, the harder it was to think of what to say. From beneath her coat collar, she pulled out the pendant that the Sorters had gifted her at Christmas. It was a lifetime entry pass to the Bureau, their hidden world beneath Royal Mail Headquarters. She hadn't used it yet, because it was easier for Wishyouwas to visit her while he was on his lost letter delivery rounds. The pendant was one of her most precious possessions, along with his letters and her special service medal from the Queen for saving the Christmas post. She'd pinned that to the inside of her coat so that it didn't get lost during the move.

Penny ran her thumb over the smooth glass of her pendant. It represented the three ranks of the

Sorters: a silver-rimmed monocle, the symbol of the Solvers, framed a watch dial that Wishyouwas and every other Deliverer wore around their necks. The watch hands were crafted from a twisted paperclip, like the ones the Gatherers used for picking locks. Penny listened to the seconds ticking past. *I've almost run out of time to tell him*, she thought.

Just then a loud knock made her startle. She slipped her pendant out of sight and slid the lid back on to the shoebox as the door opened.

'You all right, Pen?' Uncle Frank asked. He peered into her room, leaning on his walking stick. His ginger eyebrows furrowed. 'You've been a wee bit quiet.'

Penny gave him a small smile. 'I'm fine, just packing my last things.'

'Want me to take that oot to the van for you?' he asked, nodding at the shoebox.

'No thanks, I'll carry it. It's Wishyouwas's letters.'

'Ah.' Uncle Frank kept his mouth open, as if he wanted to say something more, but then he shut it again and tweaked one end of his moustache. 'Well, you'll still be able to write to each other when you're in Scotland,' he said finally. His voice sounded gravelly, and Penny hoped he wasn't catching a cold. There was a rotten wind blowing outside. 'I'll write to you and Nora too, and visit as often as I can,' he said, then swivelled on his stick and went out.

Penny jumped off her mattress with an echoey thud. Her bedroom was cold and empty now – no rug on the floor, no books or trinkets on the shelves, no pillow or sheets on the bed. She swallowed a sigh, and it became a small hard lump that lodged in her throat. The flat she and her mother had rented was very small and sandwiched between two other flats, with noisy neighbours, a shared outside toilet and no garden, but she was still going to miss it. Now their belongings and memories were packed inside a Royal Mail van, ready to be driven up to Scotland that morning by Bert, who worked with Uncle Frank and had volunteered. Penny took one last look, then followed him into the hallway and closed the door behind her.

She wandered into the living room. It looked

just as blank and strange as her bedroom, except for one cardboard box in a corner. Her mother was hunched over it, her face hidden by loose wisps of flame-like hair that had escaped from beneath her headscarf. She jerked her head up as soon as Penny walked in, revealing anxious creases around her eyes, and a glimpse of a sky-blue pilot's jacket, neatly pressed and folded, inside the box. Before Penny could ask if something was wrong, her mother closed the flaps over the box and tamped them down. Then she wiped her hand over her face, smoothing the lines away into a smile. 'Well, isn't this exciting?' she said, springing to her feet. 'We're almost packed. Just think, tomorrow night we'll be on the sleeper train to Aberdeen!'

Penny stretched her mouth into a smile too, and tried to feel just as excited, reminding herself of all the good reasons for moving there. Thanks to her mother's piloting experience and excellent knowledge of radios and Morse Code, she had been offered the position of Head of the Telegraph School at the Aberdeen Crown Street Post Office. It

was a prestigious, well-paid job and meant they could afford to rent a smart town house with its own garden, all to themselves. Best of all, Mum would be home a lot more. No more flight delays because of bad weather. No more missed weekends together. They'd be able to spend time exploring the country her mother and Uncle Frank grew up in. Penny *was* half Scottish after all. She belonged there just as much as in London. Her spirits lifted a little and she took a breath, trying to inflate them even more. 'It'll be great, Mum,' she said.

Uncle Frank came in and nudged the cardboard box with the end of his walking stick. 'Last one, I hope,' he puffed. 'How you both squeezed so much into this wee place I'll never know.'

'And you're sure you don't mind us staying with you at the post office, Frank?' Penny's mum asked, turning to her brother. 'If it's awkward for you we can look for somewhere else …'

'What, on a bank holiday Monday?' he replied, glancing at Penny with a twinkle in his eyes. 'Make you search for a hotel when London is crammed full of visitors for the Queen's coronation tomorrow? It's tempting, Nora …'

'Oh, you!' Penny's mum gave him a friendly shove.

'Besides, I've gone to all the trouble of renting a television set,' Uncle Frank added.

Penny gasped and jumped on the spot. 'You have, honestly?' She'd never watched a television before, only seen them through the windows of expensive shops.

Uncle Frank nodded and lifted his chin higher. 'You'll be able to watch the Queen being crowned *as it happens*,' he said. 'It'll feel just as if you were inside Westminster Abbey. We'll have a celebration. It can, ah, double up as your leaving party,' he said, his voice going gravelly again. 'Well, I'd better get this in the van.' He propped his stick against the wall and bent down to pick up the box.

'Let me help you, Frank.' Penny's mum took two of the corners. 'You shouldn't be carrying so much with that leg of yours.'

'Och, stop fussing!'

Their voices faded into the hallway. Penny took the stick for her uncle and turned to leave with her box of letters. She had just reached the doorway when a sudden thud from behind made her jump. She spun around, her shoulders tensed.

Something had fallen into the fireplace, sending up a puff of old soot. A small dark ball wriggled and writhed in the grate, as if a piece of coal had come alive.

A pigeon or a small crow, probably, Penny thought. Her shoulders relaxed. She could hear the wind wailing down the chimney. The poor thing must have taken refuge on the roof and lost its balance. Penny set down the box and walking stick, and knelt close to the grate. Slowly, so as not to frighten it, she cupped her hands and reached forwards to catch it …

Without warning the dark ball hopped out of the grate on to the floorboards, looking strangely misshapen for a bird. Penny flinched and pulled her hands back as it shook itself and sneezed, emitting a tiny black cloud. Then it uncurled, and two big,

round, moon-bright eyes cracked open in a filthy but familiar face. It blinked at her. 'Hello, Dear Penny!'

'Wishyouwas!' Penny cried, staring at how strange he looked. Then she thrust her hands out. The little Deliverer bounced into her open palms, smudging them all over with dirty, long-toed paw-prints, but Penny didn't care.

Wishyouwas opened his mouth and tried to speak, but instead let out an even louder sneeze. He wiped his face with a paw, which only made it grubbier. 'I has missed you, Dear Penny!' he squeaked.

Penny hugged him to her cheek and a happy shiver went through her as his velvety paws clasped her neck. She had really missed him too. 'Why didn't you come in through the letterbox like you normally do?' she asked, holding him out in front of her. 'Only Mum and Uncle Frank are here. They're just outside ...' She glanced behind her, and stiffened. What if Wishyouwas saw the empty room and guessed she was moving? He'd be terribly hurt that she hadn't told him. Penny turned back and faltered, trying to think of how to explain, but before she could say a word Wishyouwas beckoned her closer and his whiskers tickled her cheek. He whispered quickly in her ear.

'I runned over the roofs because it is faster. I has urgent, secret business and has come to ask for your help, Dear Penny.'

'*My* help?' Penny whispered back. For the first time all day, she felt a real tingle of excitement and forgot what she had been going to say. 'What's it about, can you tell me?'

Wishyouwas nodded and reached over his shoulder, where a cardboard toilet roll was strapped on to his back with parcel string. Penny knew he used it sometimes for protecting lost letters from bad weather. He reached into it and pulled out a tightly rolled envelope. But as he straightened it out, Penny saw at once that it wasn't a lost letter. Instead, the envelope was addressed to him:

Wishyouwas, LLB, London

'LLB' stood for the Lost Letter Bureau, the official name for the Sorters' home – Penny used the same address herself when she wrote to him. But this wasn't one of her letters. 'Who's it from?' she asked.

Wishyouwas didn't answer. Instead he gave her the letter and hopped to the floor, nibbling the tip of one of his long, twig-like fingers.

As soon as Penny opened the letter, she caught her breath. Printed at the top of the paper was Queen

Elizabeth's royal cipher – *EIIR* – above the words, 'From Her Majesty's Private Office'. The letter was written in a very neat, human hand, and read:

Wishyouwas,
    You are hereby summoned on an urgent, confidential matter to Her Majesty's Office at Buckingham Palace. Please attend punctually at three o'clock in the afternoon on Monday, 1st June.
    L.V.

Penny's breath whooshed out of her. 'That's today. I wonder why the Queen wants to see you?' she asked Wishyouwas, and then spotted the time on the watch dial medallion hanging around his neck. 'But it's already two o'clock!' she gasped. 'You have to go.'

Wishyouwas's back paws remained rooted to the floor. The tips of his ears quivered. 'What if … what if I is going to be downgraded again?' he squeaked.

It was such a silly worry that Penny snorted. But Wishyouwas's eyes widened to the size of shillings. She remembered the terrible time he had been downgraded by the Sorters' rulers, in punishment for getting caught while gathering a pretend lost letter she had written. So she added more kindly, 'Of course you won't be. The Queen herself upgraded you to a First Class Deliverer. You're a hero.'

'I isn't any more. Sometimes …' Wishyouwas looked down and clutched his Deliverer's medallion as if he were scared it might sprout wings and fly away. 'Sometimes I is late delivering lost letters because I readed the address wrong. And Deliverers always has to be on time.' He looked up at her and clasped his paws together. '*Please*, Dear Penny, come with me! If you is there too, then maybe the Royal Postmistress is remembering the good things we done before, and forgiving me.'

'I'm *sure* you don't need to worry …' Penny trailed off as a horrible thought struck her. This might be their last time to see each other. And what if he *was* in some kind of trouble? If there was any chance she could help him, she had to try while she still could. 'All right, I'll ask my mum,' she said, jumping to her feet.

'Wait, Dear Penny!' Wishyouwas sprang forwards and yanked her shoelace, pulling her back. 'The letter says it is confidential. That means I isn't supposed to tell anybody. I isn't even supposed to tell you, but you is my best friend.'

Penny felt a big, warm bubble swell inside her chest. 'How about saying we're going to visit the Bureau?' she suggested. 'If we go there after Buckingham Palace, then it'll be true.'

'Thank you, Dear Penny!' In one giant leap Wishyouwas sailed through the air and landed on her left shoulder. He wobbled and clutched her ear for balance, a small frown creasing his face. 'You is different,' he said.

Penny flicked her black hair. It swished just below her chin. 'I had it cut for my eleventh birthday,' she said, before realising what he really meant. 'Oh, now you can't hold on to my plait. Hang on, I have an idea.' She picked up the box and walking stick from the floor and then went out into the hallway. Her old school satchel was hooked beside the front door, packed with her nightie, toothbrush and a few other things to use at Uncle Frank's. 'I could carry you in this, if you don't mind?' she suggested, holding the flap open. 'That way nobody will see you.'

Wishyouwas slithered down the strap, leaving a long streak of soot, and nestled himself snugly between two pairs of socks. Then Penny opened the front door, letting in a great gust of wind. A Royal Mail van was parked outside, its back doors held open by Bert in his postman's uniform. He gave her a grin and a wave, then lurched to stop the door banging shut in the wind.

Hermes, Uncle Frank's adopted greyhound, bounded over, barked and snuffled at Penny's satchel. Wishyouwas poked his grubby head out and patted him on the head.

'Hello, wee fellow!' said Uncle Frank. '*Down*, Hermes.'

The greyhound gave Wishyouwas a long lick, washing his fur clean but making it stick up at funny angles. Penny laughed. It was hard to believe he was the reason Wishyouwas only had half a tail.

Hermes was a different creature entirely from the poor, mistreated hunting dog he had once been.

As Penny hoped, her mother was happy to let them go. Her eyes softened at the small Sorter. 'All right, seeing as it's your last chance,' she said, and Wishyouwas's head tilted at Penny in a questioning way. 'Just make sure you stick together and stay at the Bureau until morning.' She gazed at the sky with a pilot's eyes. 'I don't trust this weather. I feel a storm coming.'

Uncle Frank nodded. 'Telephone the post office if you run into any trouble. The number is POST-1516.'

'We will. Thanks!' Penny said. She gave Uncle Frank his stick and the box of letters, then hurried away just in case they mentioned anything more about moving. She'd tell Wishyouwas everything when they arrived at the Bureau, she decided as she ran. Then she could say a proper goodbye to her other Sorter friends too. It had been so long since she had seen Thiswayup, the wise old Solver for whom nothing was impossible, and shy, brave little

Withlove. She even missed the twin guards Fragile and Handlewithcare, with their gruff, tough manners. But for now, she pushed that thought to a corner of her mind. She wanted to cling on to the happy, bubbly feeling of being with Wishyouwas for as long as possible.

She raced to the bus stop, trying not to bump Wishyouwas too much in her satchel. A red double decker arrived almost at once.

'Where are you off to, miss?' asked the conductor as Penny clambered aboard.

'Buckingham Palace, please,' she said breathlessly.

'To see the Queen?' he asked with a chuckle, whirring off a ticket. Luckily, he moved on and asked no more.

2

Always on Time

Leaves zipped past the bus window and gulls hovered high on the strong air currents as the double decker rattled over Vauxhall Bridge. Penny and Wishyouwas pressed their noses to the glass.

'I hasn't never been on a bus before,' Wishyouwas squeaked softly. He wriggled further out of the satchel to see better, his round eyes shining.

Penny had, but London still seemed different and exciting. It looked as if the whole world were pouring into the city to see the Queen's coronation. Smoke billowed up around them like fog as steamships chugged beneath the bridge, their multicoloured flags hailing from countries she didn't know the names of. Along the streets, every shop was festooned with fluttering red, white and blue bunting. Their windows displayed celebration biscuit tins, tea towels and plates. Tourists swarmed everywhere, clutching suitcases, cameras and fluttering maps, asking questions of bewildered-looking police officers. A sense of tingling anticipation was in the air, giving her goosebumps.

As the bus trundled along The Mall towards Buckingham Palace, Penny saw tiers of wooden benches being erected for the crowds to watch the royal procession on Tuesday. And then, at the end of the long road, the beautiful, white-pillared palace came into sight.

Wishyouwas squirmed further and further out of the satchel, until suddenly he tumbled out and landed on the shoes of a lady sitting beside Penny. The lady's eyes lowered, and doubled in size as Wishyouwas righted himself. Then her feet shot into the air with such force that a suitcase she had been holding crashed into the aisle. It popped open, spilling out dresses and blouses and stockings. '*Un ratto!*' she shrieked, flapping her hands in the air.

Wishyouwas dived out of sight beneath a frilly blouse. At the same time Penny leaped up and squeezed past the lady, trying not to trample on her clothes, and fled to the front of the bus. She felt Wishyouwas scramble up her coat and drop into the satchel like a stone, but even so the lady continued to shout and point in their direction, rattling off words faster than a typewriter and making everybody stare. Penny grimaced. She didn't speak the lady's language but understood exactly what she had meant. Though all the Royal Mail employees knew about the Sorters and how special they were, most ordinary people never looked beyond their brown fur, worm-like tails and darting paws.

The bus hissed to a stop. While the conductor tried to calm the lady, Penny hopped off the footplate and ran along the pavement, trying to put as much distance between them and the bus as possible. *We'll have to be extra careful with so many people about*, she thought. She weaved through a ring of tourists and accidentally scattered a flock of pigeons being fed seeds and sandwich crusts. A particularly podgy pigeon with goggle-like markings around its eyes landed on a man's bowler hat and cooed, much to the crowd's delight, but Penny didn't stop to watch. As she drew closer to Buckingham Palace, the tourists became too many to pass easily. Despite the windy weather, a crowd at least three-people deep jostled for view, their big cameras flashing. Small children sat on shoulders, so that Penny couldn't even see the gates. She lowered her head and opened her satchel.

'How are we going to get in?' she whispered. 'Did the letter come with any instructions?'

Wishyouwas shook his head. He peeked out at the crowd and his ears drooped. Clearly he hadn't thought of this predicament either. At Christmastime they'd arrived by police car and been escorted inside the palace by a butler. Penny bit her lip. It was strange the Queen hadn't said *how* he should get in. Maybe she imagined that, being so small and quick, Wishyouwas would easily sneak inside the palace without being spotted. But there was no way Penny could. Plus, she wasn't invited. 'You go in,' she said to Wishyouwas. 'I'll wait for you here.'

Wishyouwas clung to the strap of her satchel and shook his head. 'I is NOT going in without you,' he insisted, puffing out his cheeks. 'We promised we would stick together.'

Penny glanced at his watch dial. It was already ten minutes to three. 'But you can't be late. Like you said, Deliverers must always be on time.'

Wishyouwas's nose scrunched stubbornly. 'I is finding us a way in.' He dropped to the ground and began to hop and jump between the gauntlet of legs, leading Penny slowly around to one side of the palace. She squirmed past people, trying to keep his small, scurrying body in sight. Another three minutes passed before they reached a spot where the crowd was thinner and they found a gap to peer through the wrought-iron railings. Wishyouwas clambered on to her shoulder, hunching low to stay out of sight. On the other side was a wide court-yard, and behind that an archway that led inside the palace. Two royal guards wearing matching red jackets stood as rigid as pencils in sentry boxes either side of the arch, rifles hooked over their shoulders. Their black busby hats were pulled low over their noses and they looked exactly alike, except one guard had a chestful of medals. Surely even a Sorter couldn't sneak past them without being spotted, Penny thought. But there wasn't time to find another way. 'You *have* to try, Wishyouwas,' she urged him. 'I can't—'

She jumped as a motor car honked its horn and drove under the archway, exiting the palace. To Penny's right, two tall gates began to swing inwards automatically to let it through. The crowd craned their necks as the gleaming car purred past them, and then a collective groan went up when nobody could see through its tinted windows.

'The Duke of Edinburgh, perhaps?' a man close to Penny said in a hopeful voice. 'Or maybe even the Queen herself?'

But Penny wasn't watching. Instead she stared at the open gates. A desperate idea took hold of her. She might get into a whole heap of trouble, but whatever happened she couldn't let Wishyouwas be late to see the Queen. Then he really might be downgraded. She sucked in a sharp breath to squash down her nerves. 'Wishyouwas, can I borrow your letter?'

He passed her the rolled-up envelope at once. 'What is you thinking, Dear Penny?'

'I'm going to get you in!' she said, hastily removing the letter and flattening it out. 'As far as I can anyway. Then you'll have to run for it.'

Wishyouwas frowned and opened his mouth to say something, but the palace gates had already begun to close. 'Stay in the satchel!' Penny warned. She felt him shimmy down her arm and wriggle out of sight as she wormed her way between people to stand just outside the gates. They were almost closed ... The tourists began to fan out again ... *Now!*

She jumped sideways through the narrow gap, then with a tingle of fear up her spine she sprinted for the archway. The gates clanged shut behind her and astonished shouts burst from the crowd. In front of her, the guards in the sentry boxes leaped to life and made an X with their rifles to bar her way. They reminded Penny of the Sorters' guards, Fragile and Handlewithcare, only a hundred times bigger. 'Halt, in the name of the Queen!' the guard with the medals bellowed.

Penny skidded to a stop. 'Please,' she panted, 'I have to go in!'

'You have five seconds to explain yourself before we arrest you as an intruder,' he barked. 'And I'm only giving you that chance because you're so young. Five!'

Penny waved the letter in her hand. 'I have a summons from the Queen.'

'Likely story,' said the guard. 'Four!'

'It's true.' Penny thrust the letter towards him, when to her horror it was ripped from her fingers by the wind. She jumped for it, but the white paper rose like a kite in the air.

'Three!' boomed the guard.

Penny watched, helpless, as the letter fluttered over the roof of the palace.

The guard, however, didn't take his eyes off her for a second. 'Two!'

Penny glanced down at her satchel and silently willed Wishyouwas to run, but he was still hiding, not wanting to go in without her. Her chest tightened with guilt.

'One!' The guard stepped forwards and reached out a hand to grab her. As he moved his medals flashed – and Penny had a sudden brainwave. She dug inside her coat.

'HANDS IN THE AIR!' the guards roared together. They swung their rifles towards her.

Penny lifted her trembling hands and at the same time held up her silver medal.

The guards stiffened like nutcrackers. Their busby hats came down so low that Penny couldn't see their eyes, but she sensed the one with the medals was peering forwards. 'What the blazes are *you* doing with a Special Service Medal?' he spluttered.

'It's mine,' she said.

'Balderdash!'

'I promise it is,' she said in a rush. 'The Queen awarded it to me at Christmas. Take me to see her and ask yourself if you don't believe me.'

The guards glanced at each other.

'You said the letter was a *summons*?' asked the guard with the medals.

Penny nodded. 'On royal paper with the Queen's cipher at the top.'

'Who was it signed by?'

For a moment Penny's mind went blank. She closed her eyes and tried to picture the initials at the bottom of the message. 'L ... L.V.?' she said. But she had no idea what they stood for.

When she opened her eyes, to her complete amazement the guards had shouldered their rifles. The guard with the medals jerked his head at the archway. 'Show her in,' he ordered. 'Quickly, before this incident becomes front page news!'

The other guard swung smartly round with a snap of his heels.

Penny blew her breath out and stumbled after him, trying not to grin with relief. She could hear the crowd murmuring behind her, though their voices faded as she walked beneath the archway. On the other side, she felt her eyes widen. It wasn't what she'd expected at all.

A large square was surrounded by columned buildings three storeys high. But instead of a palace, it looked more like an ordinary shopping street. On one side, a row of cosy shops had gold-painted signs hung above their doors. Penny saw a grocer's, a baker's, a butcher's, a hairdresser's, a bank, even a post office with a telephone booth and a postbox outside it! She longed to show Wishyouwas, but he was staying out of sight. He needn't have, for it was a holiday and the shops were shut. The guard led her across the square, away from the shops towards a series of numbered front doors. He pressed a buzzer beside one of them. After a few moments it clicked open, and he directed Penny inside.

As Penny stepped through, she instantly wished she'd worn a smarter dress, or had a chance to brush her hair. Now it felt like a palace again. The corridor ahead was wallpapered in silvery swirls and the grey carpet was so plush that it silenced the sound of the guard's shiny boots. He led her past gilded paintings of birds of prey, illuminated by crystal chandeliers. Then they reached a wide, winding staircase and all the way up to the top landing, where a huge grandfather clock ticked. The guard turned along another corridor, before stopping outside the last room. 'Knock and wait to be allowed in,' he said, before turning on his heel and marching away.

'We're here,' Penny whispered. 'You can come out now.'

The satchel wriggled and Wishyouwas dropped to the carpet beside her. He licked his paws and flattened his sticky-up fur, still smudged with soot.

'Ready?' Penny whispered.

'I think I is,' he said, although his voice was a little squeakier than usual.

Penny took a breath and knocked twice.

'Enter!' called a woman's voice faintly from inside the room.

A gust of cold air blew past them as Penny opened the door. An enormous sash window was half open inside the room, with waving tree tops visible outside. The next thing Penny noticed was a large wooden desk, and a head of soft brown curls bent over it, adorned with a hairclip of mottled grey feathers. Penny could hear the scratching of a nib on paper, along with the ticking of a cuckoo clock upon a wall. She didn't dare speak and interrupt the Queen while she was at work. Perhaps this was her private office? She looked down at Wishyouwas, who had his paws clenched tightly together and seemed to be trembling slightly, though it might have just been the wind through his fur. The breeze ruffled a grey feather boa draped over a hatstand in the corner, moving it to and fro like a fluffy snake.

A loud *scrunch* came from the direction of the desk, and a pale hand with silver-varnished nails dropped a ball of paper into a half-filled wastepaper basket. 'Oh drat, an ink spot. I do so detest mistakes,' murmured a voice.

Penny curtsied at once. 'Hello, I mean, um … Good afternoon, Your Majesty,' she said.

'Good afternoon, Dear Royal Postmistress,' added Wishyouwas in a muffled voice. He bowed so low his nose was buried in the carpet.

'Ha ha!'

It was a most peculiar, high-pitched laugh. Penny looked up and felt the blood rush to her face. Wishyouwas straightened and let out a surprised squeak.

'I'm so sorry!' Penny said. 'We thought you were … The letter said—'

'There is *no* need to apologise. People make the same mistake all the time!' said the lady. She stood up in a grey satin dress that shimmered in the light. A silver fountain pen dangled from a chain around her neck. 'I take it as a tremendous compliment when people think Her Majesty and I look alike. Almost like birds of a feather, ha ha!' She was around the same age as the Queen, Penny thought.

But her nose was longer and sharper and her eyes were a cool, cloudy colour, not summer-sky blue like the Queen's. The only thing that wasn't grey about her was her vivid red lipstick. 'My name is Lady Vellum,' she introduced herself. 'I am the Queen's Royal Secretary.'

'Oh, you're L.V.!' Penny said as the initials on the summons suddenly made sense. 'I'm sorry, I lost the letter in the wind ...'

At that moment a cuckoo burst out of the clock on the wall, making her and Wishyouwas jump. 'Do not worry about that,' said Lady Vellum with a wide smile. 'What matters is that, as one expects of a First Class Deliverer, you are *exactly* on time, Wishyouwas,' she said, her grey eyes gleaming at the tiny Sorter.

3

For Sorters' Eyes Only

Lady Vellum walked around her desk and crossed the carpet in pencil-sharp grey stilettos. She leaned over Wishyouwas, and her fountain pen swung like a pendulum on its chain. 'What an adorable little thing you are!' she said. 'The Sorters are a national *treasure*.' Wishyouwas hopped out of the way as the pen whisked past his nose. 'And you –' Lady Vellum straightened and shook Penny's hand with the tips of her fingers – 'must be Miss Penelope Black. How splendid of you to come.' She smiled, without any hint that Penny was uninvited.

'H-how do you know who I am?' Penny stammered.

'I know *everyone* of interest to the Queen,' said Lady Vellum. 'It is my job as Royal Secretary to correspond with everybody – from Presidents to Post Guardians! I write all Her Majesty's official letters.' She turned her gaze on Wishyouwas. 'Including the missive summoning you here.' She returned behind her desk and closed the window. 'There. We wouldn't want you getting snatched

away on the wind, would we? Ha ha! Please make yourselves comfortable,' she added.

Penny pulled up a velvet-covered chair and Wishyouwas hopped on to the very edge of the desk, his chest sucked in. He seemed to be holding his breath.

'Excuse me, Lady Vellum, but when is the Queen coming?' Penny asked.

'The Queen?' repeated Lady Vellum, sounding amazed. She sat opposite them. 'Oh dear, did you imagine you would be seeing her today? I am afraid Her Majesty is far too busy with final rehearsals for the coronation tomorrow. She departed for Westminster Abbey just a few minutes ago, in fact. I am here in Her Majesty's place. I am afraid there is a rather delicate and unpleasant matter I must discuss with you.'

Penny glanced at Wishyouwas, and for the first time worried he might be right: what if he *was* in trouble? Beneath the soot, his fur paled. He reached out and clutched her finger. Then finally his courage seemed to snap. 'Is – is I to be downgraded, Dear Lady?' he blurted.

Lady Vellum blinked. 'Downgraded?' she asked. 'Whatever do you mean? You were summoned here, Wishyouwas, as an envoy for the Lost Letter Bureau.'

Wishyouwas gradually returned to his normal colour, but his toes still twitched with uncertainty. 'What is an envoy?' he asked.

'A trusted messenger,' Lady Vellum replied. 'I must give you a very important message to carry back to the Lost Letter Bureau.'

Wishyouwas suddenly stood so straight on his paws he looked like he would lift off the desk. 'What message is you wanting me to deliver, Dear Lady?'

'One that is top secret and *strictly* for Sorters' eyes only,' Lady Vellum replied. 'However, I see no reason to exclude you from that category, Miss Black.' She turned her grey gaze on Penny, and smiled. 'Her Majesty trusts you. So, therefore, shall I.'

Penny felt a swell of pride and sat up straighter too.

Then Lady Vellum leaned across the desk and beckoned them closer. In barely a whisper she said, 'You must commit this message to memory, for I fear to write it down in case others might read it. You must also promise not to mention what I am about to tell you to *anyone* outside of the Bureau. Not even to your own family, Miss Black.' She paused and looked at them in turn.

Penny swallowed and nodded. Wishyouwas nodded too, his eyes wide and ears pricked forward.

Lady Vellum began to twirl her silver fountain pen between her fingers. 'First I must tell you why your task is so important. For almost nine hundred years, it has been the tradition for the King or Queen to write a special letter called the Monarch's Seal. It is addressed to the future monarch, telling them everything they need to know when they ascend the throne. On their coronation day, moments before the crowning ceremony, the King or Queen breaks the seal and opens the letter. Then, and *only* then, may they read it. The last Monarch's Seal was written by the Queen's father, King George.

It should have been delivered to Westminster Abbey last night, in good time for the coronation tomorrow.' Lady Vellum paused. 'However, it never arrived.'

Penny suddenly thought of the letters her own father wrote home from France, before he died during the war. Her mother had kept them all safe, just like Penny kept Wishyouwas's letters. 'The Queen must be very sad,' she murmured.

Lady Vellum raised her eyebrows. 'Yes, I imagine Her Majesty must be,' she said. 'But far more importantly, the Monarch's Seal could be extremely dangerous in the wrong hands. Just *think* of the secrets it could contain.'

Penny's cheeks flushed with embarrassment. Of course, the Monarch's Seal was more than just a letter. It probably contained maps of where treasure was stored, and special codes and things – everything the King thought the Queen needed to know!

'Where did it get lost?' she asked.

'*Lost?*' Lady Vellum said. 'If only that was all it

were!' She sighed. 'Alas, I fear that the letter was not lost but stolen. Since Christmas there have been suspicious signs at the palace. Missing mail, envelopes arriving already opened, that sort of thing … The palace postal staff and security services are searching high and low, of course, but so far have come up empty-handed. And lost letters – even stolen ones – are the Sorters' speciality, so naturally Her Majesty has requested your help. Not only is the Monarch's Seal top secret, but it *must* be found in time for the coronation, or without it the ceremony will be incomplete. The safety and future of our country are now pinned on the Sorters finding it in time.'

Penny clutched the edge of her chair as the room appeared to loom larger around her. She wondered if Wishyouwas felt as overwhelmed as she did. He had the weight of the whole country on his tiny shoulders. But his ears were tilted forwards, listening intently.

'How is we knowing the Monarch's Seal when we sees it?' he asked.

'An excellent question.' Lady Vellum traced the shape of a circle in the air with her fingernail. 'Look for a very large red wax seal on the envelope, embossed with a lion and a unicorn. The special seal is the size of a saucer, quite impossible to miss, and only *ever* used on the monarch's letters, which are written on Italian papyrus paper. These items are kept securely at the palace, so that no copies can be made. If and when you discover the letter, take it *straight* to the Lost Letter Bureau for safekeeping. With the security of Buckingham Palace in doubt, it is the safest place. Then send a message for me. Tell nobody else.'

Wishyouwas nodded, then lifted his chin. 'On behalf of the Sorters of the Lost Letter Bureau, I is accepting this message, Dear Lady,' he said.

Lady Vellum smiled at him. 'I am most grateful and relieved,' she said.

Penny bit her lip. Lady Vellum seemed so certain they would find the Monarch's Seal, but what if they didn't? Then she thought of the wise Solver Thiswayup and relaxed a little. If anyone could help them solve this problem, he could.

Lady Vellum seemed to read her thoughts. 'I know very little myself, and so cannot help much with your investigation. But I can give you one piece of information. Come with me!'

She stood up and led them out of the room, locking it behind her. Penny followed in the Royal Secretary's shadow, with Wishyouwas perched on her shoulder. On the landing they passed the grandfather clock, and the pendulum seemed to be swinging far too fast. *One day*, Penny thought. *Only one day to find the most important lost letter in the country!*

4

Mr Quilling

Lady Vellum strode across the courtyard towards the little post office that Penny had spotted earlier, positioned at the end of the row of palace shops. A small sign behind the glass door was turned to *CLOSED*, and the office looked dark, but Lady Vellum knocked anyway.

Wishyouwas crouched behind Penny's neck, his eyes and nose just visible peeping out from her hair. Penny heard a faint bang and several thuds, before a large shadow loomed behind the door and hovered there.

Lady Vellum knocked again. 'Mr Quilling,' she called. 'It is only me.'

A key rattled in the lock.

'This is the Court Post Office,' Lady Vellum explained in a hushed tone. 'Mr Quilling is the Court Postmaster. Do not worry if he is a little ... unnerving, at first. You can imagine how worried he is about the Monarch's Seal.' Just then the door opened, hiding whoever stood behind it.

Lady Vellum ushered Penny inside. The post office reminded her instantly of Uncle Frank's, where she had first met Wishyouwas. The windows had their blinds drawn, but at the far end of the room she could see a long wooden serving counter. A sorting frame with dozens of cubbyholes hung on the wall behind it, beside a huge floor-to-ceiling map of London. A single lamp shone on to the counter, which was littered with letters and envelopes. Penny breathed in. The air smelt of paper, hessian sacks and wet ink. She almost felt she belonged there ...

Until the door slammed so hard that she jumped and spun around, to face a giant walrus of a man with bushy eyebrows and a white, whiskery moustache that reached to his chin. His navy-blue waistcoat was incorrectly buttoned so that he looked a little lopsided, and his rolled-up sleeves were held up with rubber bands.

'Who the blazes is this, Lady Vellum?' he demanded in a gruff Welsh accent. His light brown eyes were sharp as drawing pins as he stared at Penny. Then his eyes slid sideways and bulged as Wishyouwas emerged into full view on her shoulder.

'May I introduce Penny Black?' said Lady Vellum. 'And her companion ...'

'A Sorter!' the postmaster puffed. 'A Sorter, in my post office, and now of all times!'

'I is Wishyouwas.' Wishyouwas stuck out his paw in greeting, but instead of shaking it, Mr Quilling glared at the Sorter without blinking.

Wishyouwas's paw quivered, then he lowered his arm and glanced at Penny with a confused, hurt wrinkle in his nose. Penny touched his paw and gave him a tiny shrug. *I don't know why he's being so unfriendly*, she thought.

'A Sorter indeed, Mr Quilling,' Lady Vellum said. She didn't seem even slightly surprised by the postmaster's outburst. 'I know that as a member of the Royal Mail, you will have heard all about them and what they did at Christmas.' She flashed a reassuring smile at Penny and Wishyouwas. 'They are here *incognito*, to deliver a message to the Lost Letter Bureau. The Sorters will help you in the search for the missing Monarch's Seal.'

'Bu— What?' Mr Quilling's mouth popped open. 'Lady Vellum, I must protest. This is a palace matter. My staff are already out there investigating every possible avenue.' He scowled at Wishyouwas. 'We are quite capable of finding it without help.'

'I am sure you are,' Lady Vellum replied, but her eyes travelled over the messy countertop as she spoke, and Penny thought she really meant the opposite.

Beneath his whiskers, Mr Quilling's face reddened

to the shade of a postbox. 'As if the Monarch's Seal were not enough, now an important key has been mislaid,' he grunted. 'I simply *cannot* allow Sorters to freely run around the palace post—'

'Then kindly protest to Her Majesty,' Lady Vellum interrupted in a calm voice. 'The Queen summoned them here.'

Mr Quilling's bluster began to vanish the moment Lady Vellum mentioned the Queen. 'I have already written a letter to Her Majesty, reassuring her that the missing letter will be found. By *my* staff,' he added.

Penny clenched her hands into balls. He seemed to think the Sorters were of no help at all. Well, they would just have to find the Monarch's Seal and prove him wrong.

'As you wish, Mr Quilling,' said Lady Vellum. 'Now, will you kindly show our friends the Red Box?'

'Well now, I don't know about that,' he spluttered.

'As senior member of the household and Royal Secretary, I *insist*.'

Finally beaten, Mr Quilling huffed and trudged across the room, his shoes thudding heavily on the floorboards. He lifted and closed the counter flap with a bang as he moved behind it. Then he pushed a pile of letters and envelopes out of the way, spilling dozens on to the floor, and lifted up a red leather briefcase that had been buried beneath them. He tapped it with his other hand. 'This is it,' he said. In the lamplight, a royal cipher embossed on the leather gleamed in gold.

'All of the Queen's letters are delivered to her in the Red Box,' Lady Vellum explained to Penny and Wishyouwas. She led them towards the counter, twirling her fountain pen as she walked. 'The Monarch's Seal was no different. After it was collected from its secret vault and brought here to the Court Post Office, it was treated as any ordinary royal letter would be. Except, of course, it *isn't* ordinary. As Royal Secretary, it was my duty to carefully inspect the envelope's special wax seal to make sure it had not been broken or tampered with, which it had not. I then placed it inside the box. Mr Quilling locked it and delivered the Red Box to Westminster Abbey.'

'Is that when it gone missing?' Wishyouwas asked.

'You tell me!' Mr Quilling barked, making Wishyouwas flinch. 'I'll have you know I was with the letter during its entire journey. The Red Box was driven inside an ordinary postal van, to attract as little attention as possible.' He swung the angle of the lamp so that it shone on to the huge map on the wall. Penny noticed a red dot in the centre, inside a rectangular-shaped building.

Mr Quilling hovered his finger above the dot. 'We are here,' he said. 'From Buckingham Palace, the van drove late at night along Birdcage Walk –' he traced his finger along a wide road backing on to a park with a lake in the middle – 'to Westminster Abbey, a journey of just half a mile.' He jabbed at another building on the map, close to the River Thames.

He paused as Lady Vellum raised her hand. 'And the traffic lights?' she asked. Mr Quilling's bushy white eyebrows formed a V as he frowned, then he looked back at the map. 'We briefly stopped here, just outside the St James's Park gates.' He tapped a spot roughly halfway along Birdcage Walk. 'Upon arriving at the Abbey, I unlocked the van and removed the Red Box.' His chest bellowed as he took a breath. 'Before giving it to the Archbishop of Canterbury, who is responsible for the coronation ceremony, I opened it again to perform a final check.' He paused and watched their faces.

Penny hadn't realised she had been holding her breath. She let it out all at once. 'And the Monarch's Seal was missing!' she said.

Lady Vellum nodded, her mouth a solemn line. 'Where it went, or who could possibly have taken it from a locked box, inside an equally locked postal van protected by trusted servants of the Crown, is a complete mystery. The letter seems to have simply vanished into thin air!'

For the second time, Penny felt a squirm of doubt deep down in her middle. Normally the Sorters solved where lost letters needed to be delivered, but this time there *was* no letter – only a seemingly impossible puzzle to solve. 'Who else knew the letter was being delivered that night?' she asked.

Mr Quilling glanced at Lady Vellum and tugged his whiskers before answering. 'Officially nobody, besides us and the Archbishop, who obviously isn't a suspect. But the palace has always had its leaks.'

Wishyouwas tilted his head. 'We has leaks sometimes in the tunnels too. We uses sandbags so the lost letters doesn't get wet.'

'Ha ha!' Lady Vellum's high laugh made Penny jolt. 'What the Court Postmaster means is that there are always *spies*. You can never quite be sure secrets are airtight at the palace.' She glanced at Penny. 'Nor are they at the Royal Mail.'

Penny felt her cheeks flush. Was Lady Vellum referring to how she had discovered the Sorters' existence? Before Penny had met Wishyouwas, they had lived in secret for generations. But, she reminded herself, the Sorters were now safer because of it.

'I am afraid that is all we are able to tell you, little

though it is,' Lady Vellum said. 'Now we must let you return to the Bureau as quickly as possible, as every minute counts. Mr Quilling, can you kindly show Penny and Wishyouwas the *other* way out?'

The Court Postmaster blinked. 'Lady Vellum, you don't mean the ... ?'

'Naturally,' she replied, one eyebrow arched at him. 'I am certain they already know the way *quite* well.'

Penny scrunched her nose at Wishyouwas. *What other way?* she thought. His eyes widened at her, not seeming to know either.

'Well, I must fly. The duties of a Royal Secretary never end! Until we meet again.' Lady Vellum leaned in towards Penny and her voice dropped. 'Leave no stone unturned,' she murmured, before patting Wishyouwas lightly on the head with her finger.

Mr Quilling politely opened the post office door for Lady Vellum. But the moment she had left he banged it shut and whirled round on Penny and Wishyouwas. 'Listen to me,' he boomed. 'I want to make myself clear as crystal.' He hooked his thumbs in his waistcoat pockets. 'Despite everything Her Ladyship might have told you, I don't want you going and looking for the Monarch's Seal. The Sorters should stay out of this.'

'But why?' Penny blurted. A surge of indignation made her face hot.

Wishyouwas's cheeks puffed out like two cherries. 'The Dear Royal Postmistress gave us this mission!'

Mr Quilling tugged on his whiskers. 'Because until I find the lost letter and prove who is behind this – and I *will* find proof – the fewer people who are involved the better. If I find you anywhere near the Court Post Office again before the coronation, I will have you arrested and locked in the guardroom.'

'That's unfair!' cried Penny, but then she felt a tug on her ear. Twisting her head, she saw Wishyouwas give her a tiny warning shake. She realised arguing might only make Mr Quilling stop them delivering their message to the Bureau. With difficulty she swallowed her anger, and nodded.

The Court Postmaster turned to face the map again and pressed the red dot in the centre of Buckingham Palace. With a scraping sound, the whole map slid sideways. Wishyouwas clenched his toes on Penny's shoulder as a dark entrance appeared. Then a string of lightbulbs flickered to life, illuminating a stone passageway. 'Off you go then,' Mr Quilling said, lifting the counter flap for them to pass through.

Penny's anger faded as amazement took its place. 'A secret entrance!' she said, peering through the opening. 'Where does it go?'

'Don't pretend you don't know that already,' Mr Quilling said. His eyes narrowed at Wishyouwas.

Wishyouwas shuffled on Penny's shoulder and his tail flicked to and fro against her neck. Penny guessed he didn't want to admit that he didn't know, not after the postmaster had been so dismissive of the Sorters. Plus, as a First Class Deliverer, he was always meant to know where he was going. He hopped to the ground and took several bounds into the passageway. He sniffed, his ears quivering like

they did when he was on high alert. Then he turned back, beckoning Penny with his paw.

As she stepped through, the cold stone gave Penny the sensation of walking inside a refrigerator. She flinched as the map wall suddenly slid shut behind them, without Mr Quilling even saying goodbye.

She stood still a moment and breathed to calm her rising panic.

'Do you know where we are?' Penny asked, her voice echoing along the passage. She walked to the top of a set of stone steps. They looked steep, getting darker towards the bottom. A gust of cool, musty air came up from below and blew her hair backwards, like a giant's breath.

'I isn't sure yet,' said Wishyouwas, which didn't make Penny feel any better. 'I only ever heared about it in stories my pa tolded me. Hardly any Sorters has ever seen it. But I remembered from the story where it goes.'

'Where what goes?'

Wishyouwas's eyes gleamed extra brightly, like two full moons. 'The Special Branch!' he squeaked.

5

The Special Branch

At the bottom of the steps, Penny turned left through a doorway and almost tripped over in astonishment.

Wishyouwas bounced on her shoulder. 'It *is* the Special Branch!'

They found themselves at one end of a small underground platform. It felt strangely familiar to Penny, even though she had never been there before. A row of open-topped train carriages the size of shopping trolleys were lined up on the tracks. The first carriage was loaded with mail sacks, and a wheeled, wicker basket sat beside it. At the front of the train a red, driverless electric engine hummed with power.

'It's the post office railway!' she exclaimed. 'What station is this?' She stared around her. There was nobody there, as if the station had been evacuated. No sign on the wall told them what stop it was on the railway line. There was an office with a glass window, but when Penny peeked inside, there was no map to be seen, just a control panel with lots of blinking buttons.

'My pa tolded me the Special Branch isn't on any human train maps,' Wishyouwas said. 'It is so secret that some Sorters doesn't even believe it is real.'

'It's real, all right!' said a loud voice.

Penny yelped and stumbled backwards. Wishyouwas fell off her shoulder and clung on to her coat collar as a woman with large, round spectacles and bushy brown hair popped out of the wicker basket. Penny backed further away while she clambered out and stood, hands on hips, wearing oil-stained overalls. 'Perhaps you'd like to tell me what you're doing here?' she demanded. '*And* whoever you were talking to. Where are they?'

Wishyouwas climbed back on to Penny's shoulder, ruffling his fur.

The woman gawped at him, blinking behind her spectacles. 'A … a Sorter! For real?'

'I is as real as the Special Branch is!' Wishyouwas said, tilting his chin upwards.

'Oh, I *hoped* I'd meet some of you one day. I've been keeping my eyes wide open ever since taking my vow of secrecy, same as all the Royal Mail staff, but I've been disappointed until now.' She wiped one hand on her overalls before sticking it out to Penny in greeting. 'My name's Pam, short for Pamela. But friends call me Spam, on account of I like it in my sandwiches.'

Spam's handshake was warm and strong. She was so different to Mr Quilling that Penny grinned, liking her instantly.

Then Spam edged closer and held out a trembling finger to Wishyouwas. He wrapped his paw around it, and Spam's eyes doubled in size. 'Bloomin' marvellous to meet you,' she said. Then she glanced at his watch-dial medallion and jerked. 'Is that the time!' Spam hurried away, talking at top speed over her shoulder. 'I transport all Her Majesty's post to and from Royal Mail Headquarters at Mount Pleasant. There's only usually one or two deliveries a day, but my train always gets first preference on the tracks. As it happens, there's some mail to send on its way now. I'll drop you off wherever you like. How does that sound?' Spam reached the office, then turned and blinked at Wishyouwas. 'You *can* speak, can't you?'

Wishyouwas looked at Penny, then nodded at Spam. 'Does you know where the burrow is?' he asked.

Spam's eyebrows scrunched, so Penny explained. 'The Bureau. It's close to Headquarters. If you can just ...'

'Say no more! The location of the Sorters is just as secret as the Special Branch!' Spam tapped her nose. 'Can't have the whole world knowing there's a postal train that goes straight under the home of

Her Majesty, can we? That's why it's only me down here.' She chuckled. 'Well, hop in then!'

Penny climbed into an empty train carriage and crouched down low. Wishyouwas curled his tail around her neck and clung on tight to her shoulder with his toes.

'Comfortable?' shouted Spam, and they both nodded.

'Then get ready to roll!' Spam grinned and gave them the thumbs up through the window of the office. She must have pressed a button, because the train lurched forwards, before taking off like a rocket into the deep, dark belly of the railway tunnels.

Penny's ears popped and everything went black. Wishyouwas's fur rippled against her cheek as the carriage rattled and shook, racing over the rails. Sparks flashed against the tunnel walls with a crackle and hiss, revealing glimpses of metal girders and spindly stalactites dripping from the roof, which barely skimmed the top of the carriage. Penny's bones trembled and the wind whipped her hair back from her face. Then, with a shocking bright glare, they whistled through another postal station, blurring past railway workers who stared as the train tore past them without stopping. Wishyouwas's back paws slid sideways on Penny's shoulder as the engine veered round a bend.

They shot through a second station. Then, just as Penny began to lose the feeling in her fingers from gripping on to the sides of the carriage, she sensed the train beginning to lose speed.

They were still in pitch darkness when the little engine finally pulled to a stop and hissed, as if catching its breath.

Penny let her own breath out and peeked over the carriage. She could hardly see her own hand in front of her face and wished she'd thought to bring a torch from home, but then she saw Wishyouwas's eyes glimmer reassuringly.

'I is able to find the way to the burrow from here, Dear Penny,' he said, turning his head in both directions.

'Is it far?' Penny murmured as she climbed out, clasping her satchel against her chest.

'Only a bit.' Wishyouwas gave her left ear a gentle tug and Penny edged her way along the wall in that direction.

She heard Wishyouwas murmuring softly to himself on her shoulder. 'Are you all right?' she asked.

He nodded. 'I is just memorising the message,' he squeaked. 'I is afraid of getting it wrong.'

'You won't,' Penny said. 'You're brilliant at remembering. I'll help too.'

Suddenly the train squealed behind them and she flattened herself between two girders. It rattled past with a flurry of sparks to finish its journey to Mount Pleasant.

In the momentary flash, Penny saw a fork in the tunnel up ahead. She recognised it from her last visit a few months earlier – it was the disused section that led to the Sorters' entrance. 'We're almost there!' she said. Then she remembered it was still the afternoon. 'Will everyone be asleep?'

Wishyouwas's fur tickled her cheek as he nodded.

'But we has to tell Stampduty and Their Highnesses the message.'

'And Thiswayup,' Penny added. 'I'm sure he can help us.'

Wishyouwas wobbled on her shoulder.

'I know it feels impossible,' Penny said. 'But we have the whole Bureau on our side.'

Wishyouwas's voice trembled. 'Dear Penny, I has something to tell you. I tried to write it in a letter, but the words all comed out wrong.'

Penny's tummy flipped over. She bit her lip. 'There's something I have to tell you too.' Maybe now was the best time, before they reached the Bureau? She took a breath for courage.

But then Wishyouwas stiffened. His ears quivered. Penny stopped, and a shiver skittered up her spine.

'Is something wrong?' she whispered.

'I isn't sure,' he said, so quietly she could hardly hear him. 'But I think something is coming towards us.'

Penny stared at the cavernous darkness before

them. She strained her ears … Was that a pattering of water droplets from the roof, or of something else, creeping towards them?

A horrible, skin-tingling memory came back to her of when a tidal wave of rats had attacked the Bureau at Christmas. But, she reminded herself, the Royal Mail had humanely removed them all. Then a worse thought made her heart stutter – Lady Vellum had mentioned spies. What if someone else knew about their mission, and had lain in wait for them to return with the message, perhaps to stop them?

'We has to reach the burrow before they sees us!' Wishyouwas said.

Penny nodded and put on a spurt of speed, half running and half stumbling. She turned right, her heart thumping, and Wishyouwas yanked on her hair just in time to stop her running headlong into a dead end. Reaching out, she felt solid, cold metal. 'Are we at the Front Gate?' she said in a shaky whisper.

'Yes, we has a new one now, after the rats broked the old one.'

The gate used to be made from the cut-out side of an old Royal Mail van, with the petrol hatch used as a little door through which the Sorters could come in and out. Penny couldn't see what Wishyouwas did next, but he leaped to the ground and after a few seconds the sound of a radio crackled to life, making her jump.

'Who goes there?' demanded a gruff voice.

'Wishyouwas, Deliverer, First Class. Dear Penny is here too. Open the gate!'

There was a long, hissing pause, but the gate didn't open.

Wishyouwas repeated what he had said, but the empty hiss went on and on. His eyes glimmered up at Penny, wide with alarm. 'I doesn't know why they isn't opening it.'

Penny fished her pendant from beneath her collar. 'I have my entry pass!' She tried knocking on the gate until her knuckles hurt. Wishyouwas jumped on to her shoulder and banged both his paws against it too, then stopped and swivelled to face the tunnel, his fur standing on end. Penny looked back and her skin prickled in panic.

Without warning the gate swung inwards. Penny toppled over, landing flat on her back. Wishyouwas tumbled in a ball along the ground.

Penny quickly rolled over, squinting in the sudden brightness. As her eyes adjusted, she sat up, rubbed her eyes and gasped.

6

Forever Occupied

'Salutations, Dear Penny!'
'Greetings!'

'Wishing you well!'

The air was filled with high-pitched, twittering voices as dozens of sleep-ruffled Sorters raced over and surrounded Penny, waving envelopes in welcome.

She looked quickly over her shoulder and saw Fragile and Handlewithcare, the twin Sorter guards, hauling on ropes woven from parcel string to lock the Front Gate. It looked very different now, made from thick metal with a round wheel in the middle, like the kind of door she imagined on a bank vault. She breathed out, relieved they were safe from whatever had followed them in the tunnels. For now, at least.

'Wake up!' she heard voices calling further off. 'Dear Penny is back!'

'Hello,' she said with a shy smile. Happiness swelled inside her. Except for the gate, the Sorters' home looked almost the same as she remembered. Brightly coloured Royal Mail posters decorated the walls above pyramids of parcel boxes. Fairy lights were strung along the arched tunnel roof like glowing droplets, along with red, white and blue bunting made out of painted envelopes on parcel string. It seemed the Sorters were also getting ready for the coronation.

Several Sorters hung upside down from the bunting, swaying as they waved to her. More scampered up and perched on top of the boxes, jostling for space so that they could reach out and shake her hands with their paws. Penny felt something sharp prick her shoe and looked down to find Fragile scowling up at her, the scar across his face scrunching his nose. He gripped a sharp letter opener like a spear in his paw, and a blue felt cap embroidered with *RM* in gold thread adorned his knuckly skull. A name badge pinned to his chest fur, once made from cardboard, had been upgraded to a smart metal pin.

'You could've given us more notice you were coming to see us!' he grumbled.

Handlewithcare came to stand beside him, clutching a silver fountain pen that reminded her of the one Lady Vellum wore around her neck. 'Then we would've given you a proper welcome party,' he added.

'Sorry,' Penny said. 'I …' She hesitated as the Sorters clustered all around her with wide, delighted eyes. *This is the last time I'll be able to come and see them too*, she thought.

'It isn't Dear Penny's fault,' Wishyouwas squeaked, jumping on to her shoulder. 'I wented to her house first.'

Penny felt a deep pang in her chest. She *had* to tell Wishyouwas about moving home. But before she had another chance, he announced, 'We has an important, top-secret message from the Dear Royal Postmistress!' An awed hush fell over the rest of the Sorters. 'We has to see Their Highnesses right away.'

Fragile and Handlewithcare snapped to attention. 'This'll mean an Emergency Audience,' said Fragile.

'I'll run ahead and inform Stampduty,' growled Handlewithcare. He slung his spear over his back and scurried deeper into the tunnel on all fours.

'Make way!' ordered Fragile, thrusting out his paws to clear a path for Penny. She felt all wound up inside, like a coiled spring. But the Queen's message was more important than her own news just now, she thought. *I'll tell Wishyouwas as soon as I can.*

At her feet, the smallest Sorters grabbed the ends of her shoelaces in their tiny paws and yanked her along, asking a barrage of questions while she stepped carefully to avoid treading on their tails.

'You'll come to our school after the Audience, won't you? It's all biggerer!' said one.

'I passed my Solver's exam! Can I show you my certificate?' asked another.

Penny grinned. 'Of course!' she said. 'I can't wait to see everything again.'

They rounded a bend and Penny ducked beneath a spiderweb of rope bridges, criss-crossing in different directions. They swayed under the weight of all the Sorters who dangled there by their paws to see her. Penny noticed they all seemed rounder in the tummy, and their fur was glossy with good health. It was a long leap from the hungry days of eating dustbin scraps before they became official members of the Royal Mail.

The same old post office furniture lined the tunnel, forming makeshift offices for sorting, pressing and resealing lost letters. One thing Penny didn't recognise was a coin-operated telephone booth fixed to the wall. There was a stack of Post Office Directories beneath it for the Sorters to reach the receiver, and beside it on a shelf stood a jar filled with brass farthings. 'You can make telephone calls now?' she asked in astonishment.

'Of course we can!' squeaked a young Gatherer who curtsied and introduced herself as Thankyoukindly. 'It's how we ask the Royal Mail for the things we need. Then they send it all here on the trains. We Gatherers are always finding dropped coins above ground, so we never run out.'

'Look at this, Dear Penny!' piped up another Sorter, wearing a glass monocle. He waved to her from the top of a filing cabinet. 'My name is Packitcarefully: Solver, Second Class! Let me show you our latest invention – the Automatic Letter Opener. It unsticks glue, wax and Sellotape, using recycled steam power! It won't take a moment ...'

He flicked a switch on a fuse box beside him, and a sort of conveyor belt made from string, with bulldog clips holding envelopes, juddered and began to move along the wall.

Penny heard water trickling. Following Packitcarefully's pointing paw, she saw three shiny steel taps protruding further down the wall. Beneath it a series of cubicles had been made with mail sacks, looking just like little showers, with billows of warm mist rising upwards. As she watched, a Sorter emerged from one of the cubicles wearing a newspaper towel and brushing his front teeth with an ear bud. When he saw Penny he squeaked and blushed deep brown, before darting back inside the cubicle.

Packitcarefully rolled his eyes. 'Keepdry *always* has to be first in the showers.'

Penny giggled. Then she noticed the damp air from the shower was being reused to steam open the trundling envelopes above. 'That's really clever!' she said.

Packitcarefully clasped his paws together. 'Steaming letters open means we leave no traces,' he said. 'It's especially useful for opening HIVEs.'

'High Value Envelopes!' Penny said. She remembered it from when the Sorters had been trapped and forced to open hundreds of Christmas cards and letters and remove anything valuable from inside them. Every single item had been rescued and replaced after they escaped. The Sorters never stole. It was their number one rule.

They were halfway up the tunnel by now. Penny passed the Sorters' canteen, made from a brand-new refrigerator, which was still closed for the day. Beside it stood stationery cupboards stuffed to the brim with boxes, tins, and jars of chutneys, gravies, and jellies, potted fruit, tinned puddings and pies.

Next was the Sorters' hospital, housed inside a spotless white bookshelf. The shelves were stocked with piles of fresh handkerchief bandages and neatly labelled ink bottles full of different medicines. One shelf held a metal In Tray and an Out Tray. But there were hardly any patients. Just one Gatherer crouched in the Out Tray, with her back paw wrapped up in parcel tape. She leaned on a crutch made from two taped-together pencils with an eraser on the top as she waved like mad, a blue hair bow wobbling above one ear.

'Withlove!' Penny cried, running over. 'Are you hurt?'

'Just a splinter, Dear P-Penny,' Withlove replied cheerfully, her long eyelashes fluttering as she smiled. 'I am First C-Class now,' she said, patting her paperclip necklace. 'I gathered a lost letter from an old chest inside a m-museum.'

Wishyouwas bounced on to the box beside her. 'Withlove is the bravest Gatherer in the whole burrow,' he said, with his tiny chin in the air.

'Our job is m-much safer now that the Royal Mail knows about us,' Withlove said modestly. 'It has been m-months since any Sorter had a serious injury.'

Penny thought again of Thiswayup. The ancient, biscuit-obsessed Solver had lost one of his legs when he was younger. So far she hadn't spotted him.

'Have you seen Thiswayup anywhere?' she asked.

Wishyouwas's fur paled to the colour of weak tea. He glanced at Withlove and she nodded back at him. 'I is showing you, Dear Penny.' He leaped to the ground and said something to Fragile, who nodded and began ordering the other Sorters to carry on towards Their Highnesses' postbox.

Penny said goodbye to Withlove and followed Wishyouwas along a side tunnel, up to an old wooden sorting frame. It contained dozens of cubbyholes, where the Solvers deciphered lost letters. When Penny first met Thiswayup, he had been fast asleep, snoring in his messy cubbyhole. She slowed her steps and walked on tiptoe, so as not to startle him awake, but as she reached the sorting frame and saw the bottom-most cubbyhole on the right, she stopped completely, and sank to her knees.

Thiswayup's cubbyhole was swept clean. The metal compass he had used as a false leg was laid across the bottom. A length of red and white parcel string had been strung across the cubby and the little chalked sign beneath it now read: *Forever Occupied*.

For a few moments Penny couldn't speak. Wishyouwas jumped into her arms and tears trickled down her cheeks, wetting his fur as he hugged her.

'He's gone, isn't he?' Penny finally said, in a choked whisper.

Wishyouwas nodded. 'A little while ago. That is what I was wanting to tell you. Thiswayup is in the Great Postbox in the Sky now. But we will never forget him. And he never forgotted you, Dear Penny.' Wishyouwas hopped back down and scrambled

under the string. He crawled to the back of the cubby-hole and returned a moment later with a miniature parcel wrapped in paper, which he laid in Penny's palm. Her fingers trembled as she untied it, to reveal a gleaming penny coin with the Queen's head on one side. The paper contained a few biscuit crumbs and a tiny note in Thiswayup's loopy handwriting:

Never forget, nothing is ever lost that
cannot be solved x

Penny wiped her eyes and smiled. Without Thiswayup's help, the mystery of the Monarch's Seal would be a lot more difficult to solve, but it was as if he had known they would need him, and was telling them not to give up. *And we won't, I promise,* she thought, straightening her shoulders. *We'll make you proud.* She placed his gifts carefully in her coat pocket, and then stood up. 'Like Lady Vellum said, every minute counts,' she said, taking a shaky breath. 'Let's deliver our message.'

Wishyouwas nodded, and rode on her shoulder as they turned back towards the main tunnel. But before they reached the end, Penny saw Fragile and Handlewithcare run past at top speed, clutching their spears.

'That's strange,' she said. 'They're going *away* from Their Highnesses' postbox.'

Wishyouwas's nose crumpled in confusion. 'But we has to have an Audience.'

Then Penny heard faint, angry shouts coming from the direction of the Front Gate and her tummy lurched. What if someone had followed them? 'We have to help!' she said, sprinting forwards, ducking under the ropes and around the bend.

Both guards were poised beneath the gate. Handlewithcare punched the button of a small radio box on the wall beside it. 'You can't come in!' he bellowed into a wire-mesh speaker. 'For the last time, if you can't identify yourself, clear off!'

'Open the door, nincompoop!' crackled a voice from the other side. ''Ow can I give you identification when you will not even look upon *mon beau visage*?'

Penny gasped for breath. What if it really *was* a spy? Then again, what sort of spy called someone a 'nincompoop'?

Fragile's fur darkened as the radio hissed. 'What did they just say to us?' he barked.

The guards clenched their weapons, clearly bewildered and very bad-tempered.

'*Encre bleue!*' exclaimed the voice. ''Ow long must we be waiting in this smelly underground cave?'

'I've had enough of this,' Handlewithcare growled, punching the button. 'If you don't get lost, I'll pin you to a noticeboard and—'

'Wait – that's French!' Penny said. The guards and Wishyouwas turned to stare at her. 'I'm sure of it. My mum flew there a lot. She's a pilot … I mean, she was.'

'You speak to them then, Dear Penny,' Fragile said, his face the colour of burned toast.

Penny knelt as the guards stood aside. She thought for a moment, before pressing the button. 'Er … *Bonjour?*' she tried.

'*Mon amie!*' exclaimed a voice on the other side. 'We are Sorters like you and come in pieces! Let us in, *s'il vous plaît!*'

Penny let her breath out and turned to the guards. 'I think they mean they "come in peace",' she said. 'Is there something we can ask to be sure they really *are* a Sorter?'

Fragile pouted. Handlewithcare shrugged.

'I has an idea!' Wishyouwas lifted his paw. 'Ask them about the Law of the Letter. Every Sorter has to know that by heart.'

'Good idea.' Penny pressed the button. 'Can you tell us the Law of the Letter, please?'

There was a long, crackly pause, and the guards gripped their weapons even tighter.

'I cannot,' said the voice, at last. 'What if some 'uman should 'ear our secrets? But in France we say, "Sorters never … ah … *voler*!"'

Penny frowned. '*Voler* means "fly".'

'"Sorters never fly"?' growled Fragile. 'I've flown a hang-glider, I'll have them know!'

'That's no Sorter,' grunted Handlewithcare. He reached for the button.

'I just remembered something!' Penny said. '*Voler* also means "steal". "Sorters never steal." That's right!'

A loud sniff came through the speaker. 'You do not want us. We go now. *Au revoir!*'

Fragile pressed the button. 'Ah, stop getting your paperclips in a twist,' he growled.

The guards yanked on the rope, the wheel turned and the gate creaked open.

7

New Arrivals

Penny couldn't help staring at the new arrivals. Not one, but two Sorters she had never seen before waited outside the Front Gate, clutching luggage in their paws. One of them leaped inside, past the guards. 'Finally, we 'ave arrived!' he declared.

He was unusually tall, wiry and wore a boat-shaped hat made from blue letter paper. He rested a blue fabric pencil case on the ground and closed his eyes, breathing in deeply. 'Ah, I 've missed the smell of *les lettres!*' he said.

The other Sorter hovered outside a moment. She wore a pair of glasses fashioned from the bottoms of ink bottles, and a grey handkerchief knotted around her neck as a cape. Her magnified, oval-shaped eyes darted all around her as she stepped cautiously inside, carrying a spectacles case covered with foreign postage stamps.

The first Sorter opened his pencil case and pulled out a miniature wire-bound notepad with a pencil stub slid between the rings. He flicked through it at

high speed and then ran a long finger down one page.

'Heeelloooo,' he said in a long, slow voice, studying his notepad closely. 'Take us to your … measuring sticks!'

There was a confused silence. The guards glared at the newcomers, before looking up at Penny. Suddenly she understood. 'Oh! You mean *rulers*,' she said, stifling a giggle.

'Eh?' The Sorter squinted at his pad again, then threw his head back and roared with laughter. He thumped his chest. 'Oh-ho, my 'eart will burst its wrapping. *Merci, mon …*'

At that moment his laugh turned into a wheeze as his eyes travelled all the way up Penny's legs and coat, to her face. '*Encre bleue*, it is true! They 'ave joined forces with an 'uman!' He prodded his companion. 'Look, look!'

'*Si*, I have my own eyes.' The other Sorter set down her case. '*Ciao*. My name is Cartolina,' she said, pushing her glasses up her nose and rolling her *r*'s with a catlike purr. 'I come from Italy.'

Her friend twirled around, flicking his tail with a flourish. 'And I am Bonvoyage!' he cried, bowing so low that his hat tumbled off. He caught it deftly in his paw and spun it around before putting it back on his head. 'I 'ave sailed 'ere over the 'igh seas!'

Wishyouwas jumped to the ground, and was the first to hop forwards to shake their paws. 'I is Wishyouwas,' he said. 'Deliverer, First Class.'

Bonvoyage's jaw fell open. 'You are famous!' he gasped, pumping Wishyouwas's paw up and down.

Cartolina nodded and shook his other paw. 'We were trying to find the Bureau and became lost in the tunnels, until we heard voices. Little did we know we were following the saviour of the Christmas post! News of your bravery has travelled far across the sea and sky.' She looked up. 'And this means you must be *Cara Penny*?' she asked.

Penny crouched and shook her paw, feeling her cheeks flush. 'I'm sorry for staring. I didn't know there were Sorters in other countries,' she said. She wanted to ask how they had managed to travel all the way to London, but before she had a chance

Bonvoyage made a sound like he had swallowed a coin.

'Not *know*?' he said. ''Ow is that possible?'

'I've never left Britain before,' Penny admitted. 'But I want to be a pilot, one day.'

'Oh-ho, then when I tell you this, your ears will pop with *stupéfaction*!' Bonvoyage said. 'There are Sorters all over Europe! France, Italy, Romania, Spain, even ...' He stopped, consulting the stamps on Cartolina's case. 'Lapland!' he announced. 'There the Sorters ride on reindeers – it is true!'

Penny frowned, trying to remember what Felicitations, the Sorters' school teacher, had once told her about how the Sorters first arrived in England. 'I thought you were washed up here inside lost letter chests a hundred years ago,' she said.

'*Si*,' Cartolina replied with a nod. 'This is correct. But the chests did not all drift in the same direction. Some sailed to France.'

'My ancestors were great sailors, just like me!' said Bonvoyage, twirling his cap. 'I know 'ow to steer boats better than 'umans.'

Cartolina lifted an eyebrow at him and spread out her paws. 'From France, the Sorters moved to many countries. We rarely see each other, but keep in touch by letter.'

Bonvoyage nodded. 'Cartolina and I are … 'ow do we say … pencil friends?'

Penny thought about it. 'You mean pen pals?' she asked.

'*Si!*' Cartolina smiled at her. 'We also have one pen pal here. You might know him … Thiswayup?'

Penny's heart gave a painful twist, and Wishyouwas's ears drooped as he told them both the sad news.

Cartolina bowed her head and dabbed her eyes on a corner of her cape. Bonvoyage removed his cap and placed a paw over his heart. 'Ahh, we were afraid of this, because 'is letters stop coming. But we 'oped it was not true. It is why we came 'ere, to find 'im.' He let out a deep sigh and looked at the tunnel ceiling. 'May you rest in *Paradis Postal*, my dear friend.'

Cartolina laid a paw on his arm. 'We still have each other, *mio amico*,' she said.

'And us,' Wishyouwas said. 'We was Thiswayup's friends too.'

Their eyes brightened. Cartolina glanced at Bonvoyage, who gave a tiny nod in reply. 'Perhaps … *you* would be our pen pals now?' Cartolina asked them.

'Yes!' Penny and Wishyouwas said at the same time. *Thiswayup would have liked that*, Penny thought. Then she blinked. 'The message!' she gasped. 'How long have we been?'

Wishyouwas checked his medallion. 'It is nearly five o'clock,' he squeaked, springing to attention. 'We has an Emergency Audience with Their Highnesses,' he explained to Cartolina and Bonvoyage.

The visitors' ears pricked up. 'Oh-ho, I would like to see this!' Bonvoyage rubbed his paws together. 'In France we do not 'ave this royal business.'

The guards spun away from the gate. 'Follow us!' ordered Fragile.

'We haven't had this much trouble since Christmas,' grumbled Handlewithcare as he marched alongside his twin. 'Two unannounced deliveries in one day, for parcel's sake!'

Bonvoyage and Cartolina picked up their belongings and followed Penny, Wishyouwas and the guards, gazing around them as they walked. The tunnel was quiet and empty, until they reached the avenue of red, green and blue letter-boxes that the Sorters used as houses. Penny just had time to notice that none of them looked old or crooked any more, before she felt hundreds of eyes swivel in her direction.

All the Sorters had woken up by now and formed a semicircle around a red postbox at the end of the tunnel. A stack of Post Office Directories formed a platform before it, with two inkwells on top. The Sorters moved apart to make room for Penny and Wishyouwas to stand in front, and their eyes bulged like bubbles when Bonvoyage and Cartolina came into view. A rustle of surprised whispers surrounded them.

Bonvoyage rested his pencil case on the ground and twirled his hat on one knobbly finger.

'*Bonjour!*' he cried. '*Salutations!*'

'Shh!' warned Handlewithcare. 'The Audience is starting.'

A young Gatherer stood upon the platform of Post Office Directories and rang a brass bell. Before it finished tinkling, he hopped out of the way and the postbox door swung open without a creak. The tunnel fell utterly silent.

A thin, pale Sorter emerged and stood before them, as stiff and upright as the yellow HB pencil clasped in his paw. Penny smiled at Stampduty and was sure his whiskers twitched, but she knew the occasion was far too formal for him to smile back.

'All rise for Their Highnesses Dearsir and Dearmadam, Supreme Rulers of the Sorters of the Lost Letter Bureau, Keepers of the Law of the Letter, Loyal to the Royal Postmistress. All rise!' he declared.

The Sorters stood on their long legs as their rulers shuffled out of the postbox and nestled themselves on their inkwell thrones. Their fur was almost as white as the swan feather quills in their paws, and their eyes were a little mistier than Penny remembered. They blinked up at her and inclined their heads, then peered down at Wishyouwas and the new arrivals.

Stampduty thumped his pencil. 'I hereby declare an Emergency Audience in session! We have been informed there is an urgent item of business ...'

He broke off as Bonvoyage skipped up the stack of directories to the top of the platform. To loud gasps from the assembled Sorters, he grasped Stampduty's face and kissed him on both cheeks, making him splutter. He did the same to Dearmadam, who frantically waved her quill in front of her face, and then Dearsir, who seemed too stunned to move.

'It is *très bien* to be 'ere!' the French Sorter called out, spinning round to face the Audience. 'Bonvoyage is my name,' he said, doffing his hat, 'and *aventure* is my aim!' He somersaulted down from the platform and landed on his paws, to a spontaneous flurry of claps.

'You are visiting from Europe, we take it?'
Dearmadam asked, still fanning her face.

Bonvoyage spun around again, his face
aglow. '*Oui!* It 'as been a long and treacherous
journey over the ocean. But Bonvoyage is never
afraid!'

Cartolina raised an eyebrow at him. 'I came
by air from Italy,' she said. 'London is so full of
humans that it was difficult to travel on the
streets, so we found our way underground through

the drains and became lost in the tunnels. Then we had a little help.' She smiled at Penny and Wishyouwas.

Dearmadam's cloudy gaze settled on Wishyouwas. 'You seem to have a habit of gathering the unexpected, Wishyouwas,' she said. 'As you led our visitors here, you shall be responsible for them during their stay.'

'Yes, Your Highnesses,' Wishyouwas said.

'*Oui!* We would like this,' said Bonvoyage. 'In Europe we still live in 'iding. Now, you 'elp us dream that perhaps it is possible to live free from fear.'

'Indeed!' said Dearsir, his jowls trembling as he lifted his chin. 'We are the official guardians of lost letters, protected by the Royal Postmistress herself!'

'And we hear she has an important message for us,' Dearmadam trilled.

An excited buzz swept over the Audience.

Wishyouwas stiffened. Penny leaned down and whispered, 'You can do it!'

He stood fully upright, his half-tail coiled around one leg, and filled his tiny body with air. Then he repeated the message all in one go. 'A very important top-secret letter belonging to the Dear Royal Postmistress called the Monarch's Seal is gone missing and maybe spies has stolen it and we has to find it by the coronation tomorrow or the ceremony isn't able to be finished!' His body deflated.

Stunned silence followed his words, as if every Sorter were holding their breath. It was several seconds before Dearmadam spoke. 'You must be mistaken. We have all heard of the Monarch's Seal, of course. It is the most guarded letter in the whole country.'

Wishyouwas clasped his paws together. 'I isn't mistaken, Your Highnesses.'

'It's true!' Penny spoke up. 'The Royal Secretary, Lady Vellum, told us herself.'

Their Highnesses' fur turned pale as paper.

'By parcels!' Dearsir muttered. 'Then if a spy has managed to steal it, we are all in peril.' He wobbled to his paws, using his quill for balance, and motioned to two Sorters standing next to a set of weighing scales beside the postbox. 'Raise the alert level to Urgent, at once!' he ordered.

8

Private and Confidential

Two Sorters lifted brass weights on top of the weighing scales and the arrow on the dial swung to 'Urgent'. Penny had only seen it that high when the rats attacked, and a shiver skittered up her spine.

'Quiet!' Stampduty demanded, thumping his pencil. But he could hardly be heard above the shocked squeaks of the Sorters. Penny watched a shadow pass over them all as their brown fur darkened, and their round eyes darted up to a portrait of the Queen hanging behind the postbox.

'*SILENZIO!*' roared a voice over the clamour, making the Sorters jump back and hush. Cartolina stood upon the platform, holding a rolled-up envelope to her mouth as a megaphone. She lowered it and nodded at Stampduty, then jumped back down.

'Ahem,' he said. 'Yes ... Be silent!'

Dearmadam ruffled her fur. 'Please repeat the message,' she said, focusing her misty eyes on Wishyouwas, and then Penny. 'Include as much information as you can remember.'

Between them they told the story, starting from the summons letter, to their meetings at Buckingham Palace with Lady Vellum and Mr Quilling.

'Finally, we rode here on the Special Branch,' Wishyouwas said.

Murmurs started up again as the Sorters stared at each other with confused, crumpled faces.

Stampduty let out a snort. 'Impossible!' he said. 'The Special Branch does not actually exist. It is a fairy story told to babies!'

'What is this "special branch"?' asked Bonvoyage, perched upon his pencil case. 'It is some kind of tree?'

Their Highnesses squirmed. 'It does not appear on any maps,' said Dearsir. 'Its location was all the safer for being forgotten. But it does, indeed, exist.'

Stampduty dropped his pencil with a clatter.

'We have never dared to go near the Special Branch before now,' said Dearmadam. 'Especially not in the days when we were unknown to humans. We should take this as a sign of how much faith the Royal Postmistress has in us. We cannot let her down.'

Dozens of heads nodded in agreement. But Penny frowned. Mr Quilling didn't seem to have any faith in the Sorters. Why, then, did he let them ride the Special Branch? It didn't make sense … She jumped as something barged past her shin.

'Let us through!' boomed a Sorter she hadn't met before. He had a large head with thick white whiskers and carried a magnifying glass in his paw. It knocked into Wishyouwas, nudging him aside. Beside him walked a slim Solver with over-large ears and long eyelashes, carrying a roll of paper over her shoulder.

'My title is Private: Solver, First Class,' said the first Sorter in a haughty tone, bowing low to Their Highnesses.

The other Sorter lowered the paper she carried. 'My title is Confidential, also a Solver, First Class. Together we are SWALK – Solvers With Advanced Letter Knowledge.'

Private thrust out his chest. 'SWALK would be honoured to accept the mission to solve this case. We have already found one possible clue. May we share it?'

The Sorters twittered to each other, their ears pricking up. Their Highnesses nodded.

Confidential unrolled the paper and spread a map of London upon the ground in front of the postbox. Sorters hopped on to the edges to hold it flat, some sitting on others' shoulders to be able to see. Penny leaned down and noticed lots of inked black Xs marked on the map.

Private prodded Penny's ankle. 'Dear Penny, please trace the route you were told the Monarch's Seal took on its journey.'

Penny swallowed her annoyance at his rudeness. 'It began here ...' She moved her finger from Buckingham Palace, along Birdcage Walk, to Westminster Abbey further east. Her finger went right past a black X.

Private hunched over the map like a hedgehog. 'A-ha!' he cried, and held his magnifying glass over the X. It doubled in size, showing an area at the edge of St James's Park, with a label in tiny script that read: *Boy Statue*. 'Just as we suspected, a DLB is located at that precise spot!' He straightened, and stared around him with a proud swell of his cheeks.

'What's a DLB?' Penny asked.

Confidential piped up. 'DLB is shorthand for Dead Letter Box. It is not, in fact, a letterbox at all, but a small, secret hiding place where nobody would think to look. During the war, Sorters discovered and recorded their locations, to gather any lost letters left there by spies.'

Penny caught her breath. 'Mr Quilling told us the van stopped at traffic lights close to there.'

Private turned to Their Highnesses and hooked his long thumbs under his armpits with a smug smile. 'If our assumptions are correct, the Monarch's Seal could have been hidden inside the DLB, perhaps for safekeeping while the search was conducted. Little did the thief realise we Sorters know of its location.'

The Sorters began to mutter excitedly to one another. Bonvoyage sprang up and bounced on his paws. 'Let us go and look right now!'

'Not so fast, whippersnapper!' Private said. '*Some* Sorters may not look before they leap, but "Mistake Your Preparations and Prepare to be Mistaken" is our motto. We cannot afford to be caught again.' He eyed Wishyouwas sideways.

'Private makes a fine point,' warbled Dearmadam. 'At Christmas we were captured and forced to steal. We may not be so lucky as to escape again. In a case as important as this, we cannot afford to fail.'

'But the coronation is tomorrow morning,' Penny said. 'What if the Monarch's Seal is still inside the Dead Letter Box? Or, if it isn't, we're back to the beginning again.' She glanced down at Wishyouwas, who nodded back with a determined jut of his chin. 'Let Wishyouwas lead the search. I can get us there overground.'

Their Highnesses bowed their heads and muttered to each other briefly. During the pause Penny caught snatches of mutterings from Sorters speaking behind their paws.

'Wishyouwas got caught *twice* as a Gatherer, remember?'

'And he's never on time, now he's a Deliverer. What if we're late delivering the Monarch's Seal because of him?'

Penny's chest tightened. She was sure Wishyouwas could hear what they were saying, because his ears drooped lower and lower, until he looked just as hunched and nervous as when he first landed in the fire grate. The roots of her hair tingled with anger at the unfairness of it. She was about to tell them just what she thought when Stampduty tapped his pencil for silence.

Their Highnesses shifted on their inkwells. 'We believe it best if such a highly sensitive, complex mission is left safely in the Solvers' paws,' said Dearsir. 'SWALK shall lead the mission, using any assistance they require.'

'Besides, Wishyouwas will have his paws full looking after our visitors,' added Dearmadam. 'They wish to learn more of our ways here, and I am sure Wishyouwas will be honoured to remain *inside* the Bureau with them, during their stay.'

Wishyouwas lifted his chin, but Penny could see his whiskers trembling. 'Yes, Your Highnesses,' he squeaked in a small voice.

'The next Audience is at twelve o'clock. We shall expect a full report on the Monarch's Seal mission then,' Stampduty said, and thumped his pencil. 'Audience dismissed!' Their Highnesses rose from their inkwells and returned inside their postbox.

Private and Confidential marched away, followed by a line of Sorters all talking eagerly about the mission.

Wishyouwas stayed where he was, staring up at the Queen's portrait.

'Are you all right, Wishyouwas?' Penny asked, kneeling beside him.

'They is right,' he squeaked in a sorrowful voice. 'I is better not being in the lead.'

Penny opened her mouth to say that wasn't true, when Bonvoyage leaped upon her knee. 'This is *bonne chance*, eh?' he said. 'We have good luck to be stuck together like stamps!'

Cartolina hopped beside Wishyouwas. 'You must take us everywhere with you, *no*?'

Wishyouwas gave himself a shake and nodded. 'What does you want to see first?' he asked, hiding his disappointment.

Cartolina smiled at Bonvoyage, who waggled his eyebrows. 'I would like to see this "DLB"', he said. 'I 'ave never seen such a thing before.'

Wishyouwas blinked, and Penny felt a slow grin spread over her face. She lowered her voice. 'You mean we can search for the Monarch's Seal?'

'Of course!' said Bonvoyage. 'Now we are pen pals, you are members of our *société*.'

Wishyouwas scrunched his nose. 'Society?' he asked.

'The Secret Society of Very Important Post,' explained Cartolina in a whisper. 'It started during the war, to rescue important lost letters and deliver them in secret across Europe. Thiswayup was its oldest member. The war may be over, but the society continues. And now, after many years, we have a new lost letter to rescue!'

Wishyouwas's ears lifted. 'You is sure? It might be dangerous.'

'Pah! Danger is my middle name!' boasted Bonvoyage.

Cartolina rolled her eyes. 'Your middle name is Valérie.'

'Shh! That is a top secret!' Bonvoyage hissed. He turned to Penny and Wishyouwas. 'Now you 'ave to take the oath.' He put out his paw. Cartolina laid hers on top. Wishyouwas and Penny nodded to each other, then added theirs.

Solemnly, Cartolina recited:

'I swear on my stamps to honour the Society,
To rescue letters by land, sky, and sea,
And protect their secrets for eternity.'

Penny felt a thrill run through her as she repeated the words.

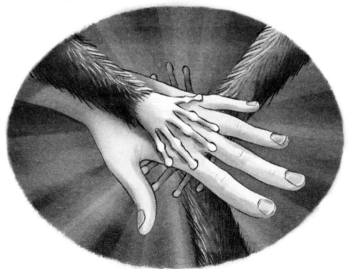

'*Voilà!*' said Bonvoyage, leaping in the air and clapping his paws together. 'So, Wishyouwas, as leader of this society mission, what shall we do?'

A sparkle returned to Wishyouwas's eyes. 'We has to find the DLB before anyone is stopping us,' he said.

9

Volantino

Penny tried her hardest not to hurry as she walked along the avenue of letterboxes, heading in the direction of the Front Gate. Cartolina gazed about her like a tourist and Bonvoyage sauntered, swirling his cap on his finger, while Wishyouwas explained what ranks of Sorter the different-coloured letterboxes belonged to. They had agreed to act as normally as possible, so nobody would guess what they were up to.

As they passed the red letterboxes, Wishyouwas thrust out his paw. 'Look, Dear Penny!' he said, pointing at a smart, freshly painted box with the number *16* printed on its little metal plate. 'This is my new home since I got upgraded.'

The mention of a new home made Penny's smile fade. A knot of nervous guilt began to tangle up inside her.

'*Bellissima!*' said Cartolina. 'May we look inside?'

Wishyouwas swelled like a balloon. 'We *is* on an urgent mission. But … if we is quick!' He leaped on top of the box, before dangling down and squirming through the letter slot. A moment later the door swung open and Cartolina and Bonvoyage jumped up to see inside.

Penny peered in curiously. She'd never seen inside a Sorter's home before. On the bottom of the letterbox was a little table made from an upturned pencil pot, with small Sellotape reels for stools. A chest of drawers constructed from matchboxes stood in one corner, and in the other was a washstand made from an inkwell, with a stamp-dampening sponge for a towel. One wall was covered in cardboard with drawing pins stuck in as hooks. Wishyouwas removed the letter carrier from his back and strung it on one of them. A hand-held torch hung like a lamp from the ceiling, illuminating the other walls, which were papered over with handwriting Penny recognised at once.

'My letters!' she said.

'This way I is always able to read your words, Dear Penny,' Wishyouwas replied.

Penny smiled. Then her eyes fell on his medallion – six o'clock already! A whole hour had passed since they had arrived at the Bureau.

'We should go,' she whispered.

Turning sideways, she opened her satchel and felt two bumps as Cartolina and Bonvoyage jumped inside with their luggage, out of sight of any other Sorters.

'Take this, Dear Penny,' Wishyouwas jumped up and detached the torch from the ceiling. Penny slipped it inside her coat pocket, while Wishyouwas also hopped into her satchel. Then she closed the door of the letterbox and turned, her heart beating faster. The Bureau was a bustle of busy Sorters getting ready for the night's work, the mission lending extra urgency to their paws. Somewhere she could hear Private issuing orders in his bossy, booming voice. Nobody was looking in her direction.

Penny quickly tried to fix every detail of the Bureau in her mind, so that she could remember it all when she left for Scotland. Then she hurried on, ducking beneath the web of ropes, which swayed from the number of Sorters running across them. Rounding a bend, she saw the Front Gate guarded by Fragile and Handlewithcare.

'Goin' already?' asked Fragile with a frown.

'When are you coming back again?' demanded Handlewithcare, a hurt wrinkle in his nose.

'I-I'm sorry, I'm not sure,' she said, squashing down a fresh pang about how much she'd miss them. But she couldn't say that, because she still hadn't told Wishyouwas.

Muttering crossly to themselves, the guards shouldered their spears and hauled on the rope to let her out. The metal gate swung shut behind her, plunging her into darkness.

She clicked on the torch. Its thin beam illuminated the black brick walls and rib-like girders of the tunnel as she walked. At the junction of the main line she listened closely, but couldn't hear anything except for the heavy breath of breeze through the tunnel.

'It's all clear,' she whispered, opening her satchel. 'You can come out now.'

The three Sorters dropped to the ground, their eyes gleaming in the torchlight.

'*Brava, Cara Penny!*' Cartolina said.

'We has to go this way,' Wishyouwas squeaked quietly, darting to the right.

Penny edged along the railway tracks while the Sorters scampered just ahead of her. After a few minutes, a crescent of light appeared ahead and a buzz of human voices floated towards them. The crescent widened to reveal a train platform with workers hurrying to and fro carrying mail sacks. A sign on the curved wall read *MOUNT PLEASANT – POST OFFICE RAILWAY HEADQUARTERS.*

Cartolina and Bonvoyage crouched out of sight

in the shadows at the edge of the tunnel, their tails flicking side to side.

'*Psst*, you must 'ide!' Bonvoyage urged, flapping his paws, but Wishyouwas jumped on to Penny's shoulder and she clambered on to the platform. Several of the workers snapped their heads round at the noise.

'Crikey, look who it is!' a man in blue overalls said, a big grin on his bearded face.

More men and women, wearing caps and head-scarves, dropped their sacks and ran over, reaching out to shake her hand and Wishyouwas's paw.

'Well I never, it's Penny Black!'

'And Wishyouwas! We'd know *you* anywhere.'

Penny heard a scuffle behind her, and turned to see that Bonvoyage and Cartolina had jumped on to the platform, darting nervous looks at all the humans.

'It's all right, you're safe here,' she said. 'Everyone who works for the Royal Mail knows about the Sorters, but they keep it a secret.'

'I thought Thiswayup 'ad lost 'is staples when he

told me this,' muttered Bonvoyage. 'One 'uman I can believe. But not so many!'

'*Si*, I never thought such a thing possible,' said Cartolina.

'On the outside it's still dangerous though,' Penny warned them. 'Most humans still think Sorters are rats.'

Cartolina nodded with a sad tilt to her eyes. 'In Italy it is the same. It is why we have learned to travel by air.'

'I'm Bill. How can I help you all?' asked the man in overalls. 'Fancy a brew? I can probably rustle you up some grub too. Tomorrow we're havin' a platform party for the coronation. There's plenty of food upstairs in the canteen.'

Bonvoyage's ears perked up and his stomach let out a gurgle as loud as a drain.

'Sorry, we can't stop,' said Penny. 'We're in a hurry.'

'Secret Sorter business, is it?' Bill asked, tapping the side of his nose with a wink.

Penny glanced at Wishyouwas, remembering Lady Vellum's warning not to share details of their mission with anyone. She nodded, but said nothing.

'Right you are. Say no more,' said Bill. 'I'll show you the way out.'

To waves from the other workers, they followed him into a lift, which rattled upwards and opened on to a car park with rows of red Royal Mail post vans, motorcycles and bicycles. Penny shivered and the Sorters' fur puffed up. Glancing up, against the darkening clouds she spotted a grey pigeon circling them, flapping its wings furiously against the fierce wind. *Mum said to stay at the Bureau tonight,* she thought with a twinge of guilt. But the sun set late this time of year. If they were quick enough, they could find the DLB and be back before darkness set in.

Bill seemed to read her mind. 'Want a lift somewhere?' he offered. 'I wouldn't stay outside if I was you. A storm's brewing faster than a kettle.'

Penny was about to say yes when her eyes fell on the row of bicycles with baskets on the front, for delivering mail. They would be able to go *and* come back fast on one of those. 'Actually,' she said, 'could we please borrow a bicycle?'

Bill grinned. 'I'll grab a spanner and adjust the seat. Be back in a jiffy.'

The moment he was out of sight, there was a sudden flurry of feathers and the pigeon landed – or rather skidded – on the concrete right in front of them in a feathery heap. Bonvoyage yelped and leaped backwards, his hat tumbling to the ground.

'Poor thing. I hope it isn't injured,' Penny said, kneeling. The pigeon righted itself and let out a long, low *coooooo*. It blinked a pair of sunset-orange eyes at her, ringed with circular markings, almost like it was wearing flying goggles.

Penny gasped. 'I've seen it before, outside Buckingham Palace. It landed on someone's hat!'

'*Si!* Meet Volantino.' Cartolina hopped forwards and stroked the pigeon's feathery head. 'Together we have delivered many letters. I trust him with my life.'

Wishyouwas hopped closer and Volantino gave his paw a friendly peck, before dipping to the ground and scooping up Bonvoyage's cap.

Penny laughed. 'He likes hats.'

'But *that* is *my* 'at,' said Bonvoyage in a temper, tugging it out of Volantino's beak.

'Here you are!' Bill's voice called to them from across the car park. He wheeled up a red bicycle. 'I've packed some grub in the basket,' he said, lifting the lid and showing them four brown paper bags. 'Just in case you get hungry on your journey.'

Bonvoyage cheered up instantly. 'Then, *mes amis*, let us journey at once!'

10

The Dead Letter Box

Penny wheeled the bicycle out of Royal Mail Headquarters with Bonvoyage hunkered out of sight inside the basket, from which she could hear the loud rustling of paper. Wishyouwas perched on her shoulder and she lifted up her coat collar so that he wouldn't be seen. 'The map showed the DLB was at a place called the Boy Statue, in St James's Park,' she said.

Cartolina climbed on to Volantino's back and wrapped her paws around his neck. 'Follow us, we will find the fastest way,' she called, and the pigeon spread his wings and launched into the air. Cartolina's handkerchief cape billowed behind her in the wind, the same colour as Volantino's wings.

Penny pedalled as fast as she could along the pavement, while Wishyouwas kept his eyes on the sky and the small, fluttering shape of Volantino, relaying directions to her.

Her fingers began to go numb and stiff with cold as they cycled closer to the centre of London, passing different Underground Stations along the way. Today was the first of June, but it felt more like February. Even so, determined tourists were taking photographs of everything from phone boxes to bollards.

Penny smelt the salty tang of the Thames, and the daylight had begun to turn dull grey by the time Volantino dipped his wings and swerved to the west. She cycled on to a wide road fringed by posh buildings on one side, and a large park on the other. A street sign read *BIRDCAGE WALK*, beside a set of park gates. 'We is here,' said Wishyouwas, and then his toes curled on her shoulder. 'Look up, Dear Penny!'

She glanced where he was pointing and saw Volantino gliding down with his legs outstretched, coming into land. Then she saw something else and her heart stuttered: high above Volantino, hovering among the torn-paper edges of the clouds, was the dark, winged shape of a bird of prey. Penny's tummy clenched with instinctive fear. 'Watch out!' she cried, but the wind snatched her words away. Then she blinked and the bird was gone. Moments later Volantino landed on the handlebars and ruffled his wings.

'Did you see the hunter?' Penny said to Cartolina.

She nodded and pushed her glasses up her nose. 'The sky can be dangerous. But Volantino is an excellent flyer.' She patted the pigeon on his head.

Bonvoyage popped out of the basket and burped, his chin covered in breadcrumbs. '*Excusez-moi!* 'Ave we arrived?'

Wishyouwas nodded. 'We is at St James's Park. Now we just has to find the Boy Statue.'

'We should go on foot and paw,' suggested Cartolina. 'If any spies are still here and see that red bicycle, they will know where we are from.'

They looked for somewhere to hide it. The path ran alongside the banks of a marshy canal, wildly overgrown with reeds even taller than Penny. At the edge of the water, behind a straggly evergreen hedge, she spotted a crooked chimney. Peering through a hole in the hedge, she found a tumble-down cottage, with a hole in the thatched roof and shattered windows. It looked like a gingerbread house that had been half eaten and then thrown away. An enormous plane tree overshadowed it like an umbrella, hiding the cottage almost entirely from view.

'There!' Penny said, pushing the bicycle through the hole. She leaned it against a wall of ivy so thick that it almost swallowed the bicycle up, and the Sorters helped hide the rest.

When Penny squeezed back through the hedge,

she found with a jolt that she was in the middle of a crowd of tourists. Their backs were turned to her and they were laughing and pointing their cameras at something ahead. Penny ducked down, and between the forest of legs caught sight of Volantino. He waddled back and forth along the top of the bench like a soldier, turning in tight circles while holding a twig in his beak. Penny grinned. *He's creating a distraction for us!* she thought. Then she jumped as a loud voice cut through the air.

'Ladies and Gentlemen, yoo-hoo! If I may have your attention, please!' A woman with blonde hair waved a red flag on a pole. 'We are about to begin our evening walking tour.' The crowd tore their eyes away from Volantino and hushed, Penny trapped behind them. 'Just visible behind these hedges is Duck Island Cottage,' said the tour guide, gesturing towards where Penny had just hidden the bicycle. 'Centuries ago, King James the First had an aviary built in this park, to house his collection of royal hunting birds. The last birdkeeper to live here was Thomas Hinton. After he retired, the cottage was sadly abandoned, and there is nothing much to see now. Let us move on to the Boy Statue …'

Penny caught her breath. 'Let's follow them,' she whispered. Three furry heads peeped out of the long grass and nodded.

Penny tagged on to the tail of the tour group. When they reached the statue, the guide didn't mention anything about spies or Dead Letter Boxes. 'It is a public drinking fountain,' she said. 'Rather lovely, isn't it?' Water spouted from four shells on each side of a plinth, on top of which sat a stone boy cradling an urn. One of his hands just dipped into it, and his head was turned away, as if he had been startled by someone.

'On with the tour!' said the guide, once photographs had been taken. 'We shall soon see a glimpse of Buckingham Palace between the trees …'

The tourists moved eagerly away. Penny slipped behind the statue and waited until the sound of footsteps had faded.

Wishyouwas, Cartolina and Bonvoyage emerged from the treeline and they all surrounded the statue. Volantino flapped over and landed on the boy's head.

'Are you sure *this* is a Dead Letter Box?' asked Bonvoyage, removing his cap and scratching his head. 'It does not look like an 'iding place for spies.'

'Confidential said they're places nobody would think to look,' said Penny.

Wishyouwas nodded. 'There has to be a hole where the letter might be.'

'Let us split up,' said Cartolina. 'We will be faster this way. Volantino can keep watch.'

The pigeon cooed and bobbed his head.

They scattered over the old stone fountain. Penny peered into every crack and crevice around the shells. She prodded and pulled every bit of stone in case something came loose, but found nothing. Cartolina and Bonvoyage swarmed all over the statue, but returned and shook their heads.

Penny's shoulders slumped. 'Maybe Private and Confidential were wrong about this being a DLB, or perhaps the Monarch's Seal was here and has already been taken,' she said. Then she looked around. 'Where's Wishyouwas?'

Cartolina and Bonvoyage's ears pricked as a tiny, thin voice echoed from above: 'Help! I is stuck!'

'Wishyouwas?' Penny called. 'Where are you?'

'Inside this pot. I gotted in but I couldn't get out again.'

Penny ran around the fountain. There was no pot, but then her eyes fell on the urn, which the stone boy's hand was dipping into, almost as if he were pointing into it …

''Old on, *mon ami*,' Bonvoyage called into it, his voice sounding hollow. He wrapped his tail around the neck of the urn and held Cartolina's back paws while she squirmed inside. Then Bonvoyage bunched his strong legs and heaved. Cartolina, and then Wishyouwas, popped out of it like corks from an ink bottle.

Wishyouwas landed on the ground and his eyes glimmered with triumph. In his paws he held a rectangular package wrapped in a waxy fabric, tied loosely round with string.

'Is it the Monarch's Seal?' said Bonvoyage, boun-cing beside him.

Wishyouwas unwrapped it and slid a white envelope from inside the wrapper. But at once his eyes lost their glimmer. Penny saw that the enve-lope was blank, and her hope plummeted. 'I don't think it can be,' she said. 'Lady Vellum said it had a special seal.'

'Perhaps they changed the envelope?' said Cartolina.

'Open it!' said Bonvoyage. 'We 'ave to be sure.'

They found an empty park bench and hunched over their discovery. Penny glanced around them, but except for the rustle of leaves in the wind, the park was quiet. Wishyouwas carefully peeled open the envelope and slid out a single sheet of folded paper. Penny held her breath as he unfolded it.

'Eh?' blurted Bonvoyage.

The message, which appeared to be written in snippets of different handwriting, simply read:

hint   on   tree

Wishyouwas sniffed the words. 'They has been cutted from other letters and sticked on.'

'It doesn't seem to have anything to do with the Monarch's Seal,' Penny said. 'It looks more like a clue to a treasure hunt.'

Cartolina tilted her head. 'Hmm ... Perhaps the thief hid the Monarch's Seal somewhere else, and left this clue for another spy to find?'

Bonvoyage's fur bristled. 'If this is true, maybe they are coming to find it now!'

At that moment something moved in the bushes behind them. All of them leaped up and Penny hid the letter behind her back as she spun round. 'H-hello?' she stuttered. There was no answer, and twilight had fallen, cloaking the park in shadow.

Suddenly a squirrel burst out of a bush and skittered across the path.

Bonvoyage clasped his chest and wheezed with relief.

'We should leave the letter here,' Penny said in a low voice. Her skin prickled and she couldn't shake the feeling of being watched. 'We might be wrong. But if this *is* a clue to where the Monarch's Seal is hidden and the spy finds it missing, they'll know we're on its trail. We just have to stay ahead of them.'

Bonvoyage retrieved his notepad and pencil from his pencil case in Penny's satchel and quickly copied down '*hint on tree*', while Wishyouwas and Cartolina rewrapped the letter in its rainproof pouch, rolled it up and dropped it inside the urn.

Then they retraced their path to the tumbledown cottage.

It was so dark beneath the umbrella-like branches of the huge plane tree that Penny could barely see where the bicycle was hidden. She felt with her hands along the ivy-covered wall of the ancient dwelling where the King's birdkeeper had lived long ago.

Suddenly she stopped and the air flew out of her.

The Sorters ran over to her and Wishyouwas jumped on to her shoulder. 'Dear Penny, is you all right?'

'Thomas Hinton!' she said. 'The tour guide said he lived here. And …' Her eyes travelled upwards, to the canopy of the plane tree.

'Hinton tree,' said Cartolina, her eyes sparkling.

Penny grinned. 'I think we've found where the clue was leading to!'

11

The Watcher

Wishyouwas and Cartolina swarmed up the tree trunk and searched all around it, feeling with their paws inside knotholes and cracks.

'I shall search on the ground,' Bonvoyage declared.

Penny helped him rummage around the base of the tree. Its bark was a patchwork of greys and greens and browns and yellows, which peeled off in flakes and surrounded its roots like fallen feathers. She sifted her hands among them, hoping to hear the papery rustle of a hidden letter.

Before long the colours of the bark faded to different tones of grey as the evening sun set beyond the tree canopy. Every few minutes they froze as someone walked past on the path, but before long the park fell quiet except for the rustling of leaves and whispers of the reeds along the nearby lake shore. Penny heard a distant, rolling rumble of thunder and knew they had to stop soon, before the storm set in. She searched twice as hard, using her feet to sweep away the bark and leaf mould, but no letter appeared.

Wishyouwas and Cartolina jumped down to the ground, shaking their heads. 'We hasn't found nothing,' said Wishyouwas.

'We can't give up,' Penny said. Volantino landed on a branch above her head with a questioning coo. The wind shook the tree, and as the branches moved Penny spotted a kite wedged between the fork of a branch, its sharp corners poking out among the mass of rounded leaves. She jerked upright. What if it wasn't a kite?

'What has you seen, Dear Penny?'

'Up there!' she said, pointing. 'I'm not sure what it is, but something's stuck in the branches.'

Volantino tilted his head, then flapped to the branch she was pointing at. Seconds later he was back on the ground, a rectangular, waxy pouch clamped in his beak.

'It's another clue!' Penny said, and the Sorters grinned at each other, but then Volantino began a strange, jerking dance.

'The bird 'as gone mad!' said Bonvoyage.

But Penny noticed something pale and stringy wrapped around his right claw. 'No, he's caught on something. Cartolina, can you keep him still?'

Cartolina stroked the pigeon's head to calm him, while Penny carefully loosened the string. 'There, all free.' She gave the string a tug and the pouch jerked over the ground towards them.

There was no debating this time: they bunched together in nervous silence while Wishyouwas peeled open the pouch and pulled out an envelope.

This letter wasn't the Monarch's Seal either. The message inside was even stranger than the last, with four glued-on snippets:

a   ß   fal   con

'This one doesn't make any sense,' Penny said.

'Per'aps it is a code,' said Bonvoyage, shrugging his wiry shoulders. 'So nobody except another spy would understand it.' He opened a fresh page of his notepad and licked the nib of his pencil. 'I will make a copy. Wishyouwas, can you read it to me, *s'il vous plaît*?'

Wishyouwas's nose wrinkled as he read it slowly out loud. 'A bee – falcon,' he squeaked.

Penny's heart skipped. 'Wishyouwas, say that again!'

His ears and whiskers dipped. 'Has I readed it wrong?'

'No, I think you might have solved the clue.'

Wishyouwas blinked, and repeated the message. 'A bee – falcon.'

Penny grinned. 'I think "abbey" might be Westminster Abbey, where the Monarch's Seal was meant to be delivered.' She sprang to her feet. 'It can't be a coincidence, this message *must* have something to do with it!'

'*Oui!*' said Bonvoyage, his eyes aglow. 'Where better to 'ide a letter than the place it was meant to be delivered? Nobody would think to search there!'

A loud creak from the direction of the cottage made them all freeze on the spot.

'What was that?' Penny breathed. Another creak followed. *Like footsteps over old floorboards*, she thought with a flutter of panic.

They crouched in silence. After a few seconds, thunder drummed in the sky, the wind wailed and the branches above their heads swayed with a creaky groan. They all breathed out.

'Must have been the tree,' Penny said. 'Let's go to the Abbey before the storm comes. Maybe we'll find something there.'

The others nodded. While Cartolina climbed the tree to replace the pouch, Penny yanked the bicycle out of the undergrowth. She was glad to leave the eerie building behind. When they emerged on to the path, the park was empty and unlit.

It was far too windy to fly, so Cartolina and Volantino rode in the basket with Bonvoyage and Wishyouwas as Penny pedalled along the path in the direction of the gates. The back of her neck began to tingle. She glanced over her shoulder and almost fell off in shock.

Behind them on the path, a tall figure was running full pelt towards them, their long, hooded raincoat flapping like a raven's wings. 'Someone's there!' she gasped, swerving wildly and just managing to keep her balance.

Wishyouwas leaped out of the basket on to her shoulder, his legs coiled and ready to spring.

Another slash of lightning split the sky overhead. Twisting her neck, Penny saw the figure look up. For the briefest moment she saw a pale face, but darkness returned in a heartbeat and the figure stumbled off the path, vanishing into the trees.

It's just somebody trying to find shelter from the storm, Penny told herself, trying to stay calm. The hidden clues and talk of spies were making her jumpy. She pushed on, pumping her legs and soon reached the gates. She tore through them and braked sharply to avoid careering into the pedestrians hurrying along the pavement, their umbrellas turning inside out. She looked over her shoulder.

'Is anyone still behind us?' she panted.

'I doesn't see nobody, Dear Penny. I think we losted them.'

Penny breathed out, and then flinched as the sky tore open and fat, cold raindrops began to splash against the pavement.

'We've got to be quick!' she said. 'Can you find the way to the Abbey, Wishyouwas?'

He nodded, his fur darkening in the rain. He hunkered down on her shoulder. 'It isn't far, Dear Penny.' He pointed towards the river and Penny set off.

Above them, just visible in another flash of lightning, a bird of prey swooped over the park and spiralled down towards the crooked cottage with a piercing cry, too far away even for the Sorters' sharp ears to hear, as Penny pedalled hard towards Westminster Abbey.

12

The Abbey Falcon

Curtains of wind-blown rain buffeted Penny as she cycled, but she forged on with a determined grimace. They soon left St James's Park and Birdcage Walk behind them.

Rounding a street corner, an enormous gothic building loomed into sight, with twin towers that seemed to poke holes in the stormy night sky. Bonvoyage peeped out of the basket and as his eyes travelled upwards they widened.

Westminster Abbey was ablaze with lanterns and floodlights. The ancient, charcoal-coloured stone church was draped in flags and banners that beat like drums in the wind. The area at the side of the Abbey had been roped off. Marquees had been erected, which yanked at their moorings, threatening to take off.

Penny felt a small tug on her ear. 'Dear Penny, how is we going to look inside?' said Wishyouwas.

Penny stared at the Abbey entrance. Despite the storm, everyone from carpenters to clergymen were rushing in and out, seeming to be in a final panic of preparations for the coronation in the morning. It would be impossible to search the Abbey with so many people around, but the rain had soaked through her woollen coat and Wishyouwas trembled on her shoulder. If they didn't find some shelter soon, they would all freeze. They had to try.

Penny ducked beneath the rope and steered the bicycle on foot between the tents, towards the entrance. A line of large stone animal statues holding heraldic shields in their claws and paws guarded each side of the huge wooden doors of the

Abbey. Penny paused beneath a giant lion, waited until there was a gap in the flow of people, and then slipped quickly through the entrance, into a marbled porch area littered with brooms, dustpans, chairs and crates. She steered the bicycle to a quiet, shadowy corner between the doors and a stack of boxes.

Through another archway, she glimpsed rows of wooden pews inside the Abbey, and glittering candles everywhere. The high voices of a choir echoed through it, singing a soothing hymn to the deep, rich tones of an organ. The lid of the basket lifted very slightly and four ears poked out, turned towards the lovely sounds.

'Where is your pass, young lady?' boomed a voice.

Fast as a blink the basket lid fell and Wishyouwas dropped inside her coat. Penny spun round. A grim-faced soldier in red uniform and a busby hat towered over her. His moustache was like a bushy black caterpillar. 'Everyone inside the Abbey must carry an official pass.'

'I – I won't be here long,' Penny said, too startled to think. 'I just need to look for something.'

'Not likely. Only the Queen doesn't require a pass and you don't look much like Her Majesty.' He looked her up and down.

'Please, it's really important,' Penny said, stepping in front of the bicycle in a useless attempt to hide it. If the soldier demanded she open the basket ...

'Let her go, at once!' called a familiar voice.

The soldier glanced around and jerked upright. He snapped to attention as a woman in a grey dress appeared through the entrance doors and hurried towards them in grey stilettos, her brown curls damp from the rain. She carried a large handbag and a feather boa coiled around her neck. The boa writhed in the wind as if it were alive, and Penny caught the gleam of a silver chain beneath it.

'Lady Vellum!' she said, with a rush of relief.

'Phew!' Lady Vellum said, stopping. Her cheeks were flushed almost as red as her lipstick. 'I am glad I caught up with you. I spotted you on your bicycle while arriving here in a taxicab.' She looked at the guard and said in a businesslike tone, 'I am the Royal Secretary. This girl and her … bicycle have a very good reason to be here. Issue them a pass at *once*.'

'Them, Royal Secretary?'

'Ha ha! Silly me, I meant *her*,' Lady Vellum said with a snort, and a sly wink at Penny.

Penny smiled back at her gratefully. Lady Vellum knew that Wishyouwas must be close, but was keeping his presence a secret.

The soldier pulled a yellow card from inside his jacket pocket. 'You'll have to sign it, m'lady, if you please.'

A slight frown crossed Lady Vellum's face. 'How irritating. I do not have a pen with me. Do you?'

Penny wondered why she didn't just use her silver fountain pen – she was sure she had recognised the chain around her neck.

'Not on my person,' answered the soldier. 'I shall fetch one and be right back.' He swivelled on his heels and marched off. As soon as he was out of earshot, Lady Vellum stepped closer to Penny and lowered her voice. 'Now we have a chance to speak privately without that nosy guard around! Where is Wishyouwas?' Her eyes scanned the ground. 'I assume he *is* with you?'

Penny felt a warm, wet lump wriggle against her neck and Wishyouwas emerged from under her collar. He almost bowed, before stopping himself.

At that moment Bonvoyage popped out of the basket.

'*Two* of you!' exclaimed Lady Vellum. She touched his blue cap with the tip of her finger. 'What a dear little sailor hat. It is quite charming!'

'My 'onoured name is Bonvoyage, *madame*,' he said, whisking off his cap with a bow.

Lady Vellum turned her eyes back to Penny. 'I am very glad to have run into you. The Queen is *most* anxious to learn if you have discovered her letter's whereabouts.'

'Is the Queen here?' Penny asked, glancing into the Abbey.

'No, Her Majesty is at the palace, resting ahead of the coronation. But any message you have for Her Majesty you can trust with me.'

Penny took a breath. 'We haven't found the Monarch's Seal yet,' she admitted.

'But we finded clues,' Wishyouwas said.

Lady Vellum's eyes gleamed. 'How intriguing! And where did these clues lead you?'

'We found them hidden close to the letter's delivery route,' Penny said. 'We think, maybe …' She hesitated. But Lady Vellum's face was watchful and serious, and she had believed in them so far, so … 'We think the clues were left behind by whoever stole the letter, to lead a spy to where the Monarch's Seal is hidden. Someone – maybe the spy – was following us in the park too, but they disappeared.'

Lady Vellum blinked. 'Hmm … it all seems a little far-fetched. But you have certainly got a lot further than Mr Quilling and the Royal Mail. Her Majesty was right to trust in the Sorters. And I in you, Penny.'

Penny's face warmed from the compliment. 'But we still don't know where the Monarch's Seal is,' she said. 'The last clue was "abbey falcon". It's why we came here next.'

'Hmm, I cannot think what that could mean, I am afraid. But keep searching. I can feel that you must be close. And remember, as soon as you recover the letter, tell nobody and return to the Bureau *at once* to keep it safe. Now do forgive me, but I must fly. There is so much to take care of before tomorrow. Good luck!' Flashing a last smile at Wishyouwas and Bonvoyage, Lady Vellum spun round, her feather boa fluttering. She left the Abbey in the rush of other officials, leaving Penny feeling oddly lost. She couldn't think why, until Wishyouwas and Bonvoyage both jumped in the basket and hid as the soldier reappeared, holding a biro.

'Where has the Royal Secretary gone?' he asked, swivelling his head.

'Oh no, the pass!' Penny gasped. 'She left before signing it.'

'Right, well, I'm sorry but rules are rules,'

the soldier said, spinning Penny round by her shoulders. 'Come along and bring your bicycle. You'll have to leave.'

Penny's chest tightened. 'But we can't! We have to—'

'Out!'

Penny miserably took hold of the handlebars and pushed the bicycle into the stormy night. The soldier eyed her closely as she left, and she knew it was hopeless to try and get back inside. They had been so close, even Lady Vellum thought so, and now she had ruined their chances of searching the Abbey! The breeze buffeted her sideways and rain trickled down her collar. She ducked between two of the animal statues for some shelter and lifted the basket lid.

'I'm sorry,' she said. 'I made a mistake.'

Volantino cocked his head upwards and his amber eyes blinked. Then he rustled his feathers and let out a sharp coo.

'We is finding another way, Dear Penny,' Wishyouwas said.

Cartolina nodded. 'The Abbey is so big that we will need the full strength of the Sorters on our side to search for the letter.'

'*Allez*, let us return to the Bureau!' said Bonvoyage. He twisted his cap between his paws and wrung out a trickle of water. 'This British weather is *incroyable*. The sea is drier than this!'

Volantino flapped his wings in a furious flurry of feathers.

'Volantino, no! It is too dangerous to fly in the storm!' said Cartolina, but the pigeon launched out of the basket, straight past Penny's head. He began circling above them, cooing non-stop.

Penny looked up at the same time as a flash of lightning illuminated the statue in sharp relief.

She recoiled. The statue was of a vicious-looking bird, with a sharp open beak and huge, clutching claws, each talon larger than her hand. Then her heart skipped. 'It's a falcon!' she cried.

'*Encre bleue*,' gasped Bonvoyage. 'You are right!'

The Sorters jumped from the basket on to the

falcon's wings. Volantino roosted on its head while they searched all over the slick stone, feeling with their paws in the darkness and rain. In almost no time at all, Cartolina popped up from behind the shield and wiped her glasses on her cape.

'*Cara Penny*, this was fastened behind the shield.' She held out a rectangular waxcloth pouch, similar to the last two they had found.

'Another clue,' Penny said. 'But it's too wet to open it here.'

'Let us just take a peek?' said Bonvoyage. 'Otherwise 'ow can we be sure?'

Penny used the basket lid for cover and carefully unfolded a corner of the waxy covering. She glimpsed cream-coloured paper, and – in another flash of lightning – something red. Her heart stuttered as she peeled back more of the cloth, to reveal a circular wax seal on the envelope, as large as a saucer.

She caught her breath in wonder. 'It's the Monarch's Seal!' she said.

13

Return to Sender

Penny and the Sorters huddled in the shadow of the falcon statue and gathered around the letter. Penny pulled her torch from her satchel and shone it upon the seal. The red wax was embossed with a lion and a unicorn, just as Lady Vellum had described. She ran her fingers over it, hardly daring to believe they had really found the Monarch's Seal.

Even so, a shiver of excitement ran through her. Wishyouwas and Bonvoyage's eyes were shining too. But Cartolina wore a slight frown, her head tilted sideways. She leaned down and sniffed the envelope, her whiskers twitching. 'When was this letter written?' she asked.

Penny frowned in thought. 'The old King wrote it, so it must have been years ago.'

'But the envelope, if I am not mistaken, is new,' said Cartolina.

Wishyouwas smelt it too and his nose wrinkled. 'You is right,' he said. 'Something smells fishy.'

'Eh?' Bonvoyage blurted. He gave it a long sniff. 'I do not smell fish, and I would know, I am a champion sea swimmer!' He flexed his arm muscles.

'Wishyouwas means something doesn't seem right about it,' Penny said. A memory bobbed in her mind, of when she had visited the Bureau for the very first time. Thiswayup had solved the lost letter she'd brought with her straight away. With a single sniff, the clever Solver had worked out that the letter was really written by her and not lost at all. Might this letter also not be what it seemed? Either way, she was determined to help Wishyouwas succeed. 'We have to find a way to be sure,' she said. 'Lady Vellum told us to take it straight back to the

Bureau. Maybe the Solvers there can help us.' She wrapped the envelope back inside its rainproof cover and slid it inside her satchel. Then she turned to clamber back on to the bicycle – and went rigid.

In a series of lightning bolts, she saw the silhouette of a hooded figure in a long cloak outside the Abbey, standing as still as stone and staring directly at her.

'The spy!' she said in a strangled voice.

Wishyouwas leaped on to her shoulder. 'Where, Dear Penny?'

'There!' She pointed, but in the next flash the figure had vanished. 'We have to go – *now!*'

The Sorters scrambled inside the basket and Penny pushed off, leaving the statues behind and standing on the pedals to go faster. She swerved and skidded through puddles, not thinking which direction she was going and hardly able to see in the rain. She shuddered with the horrible, spine-prickling fear of being chased. Wishyouwas's tail whipped in the air beside her nose as he kept his eyes locked behind them, paws bunched and ready to spring.

Penny pedalled past Big Ben's clock tower just as the bell chimed eleven o'clock, its loud bongs echoing like extra thunder. She puffed, the wind pushing against her.

'Dear Penny, we is faster if we goes underground,' Wishyouwas squeaked in her ear. He pointed ahead, and Penny spotted the red, pillared shape of a postbox. 'But I doesn't have a lock picker no more.'

Penny's thoughts raced. 'I know! My pendant has a paperclip – you can use that!' She yanked on the brakes outside a post office. She propped the bicycle against the door and gave Wishyouwas her Sorters' VIP entry pass. While Cartolina kept watch, Bonvoyage helped Penny scribble a hasty note on a sheet of his notepad: *Sorry to leave this here, please return to Mount Pleasant. Thank you.*

When she turned round, Bonvoyage and Wishyouwas were perched inside the empty postbox. Volantino let out a mournful coo from the basket, so Penny lifted him in her arms and he nestled against her coat.

'I have not seen the spy, *Cara Penny*,' said Cartolina, jumping in last. 'We have outrun them, I think.'

But now they'll know we found the letter, Penny thought. They had to reach the Bureau, where they would be safe. She scrambled inside the postbox, pulling her knees up to her chest, and closed the door.

'Why are we in 'ere?' wondered Bonvoyage. 'Are we 'iding?'

Penny shook her head. 'This is the secret way to the tunnels.'

'Eh? What secret way?'

Wishyouwas scuffled near her feet and tugged.

'Wahhhhhh!' Bonvoyage let out a long, warbling shriek as with a *whoosh* the postbox floor collapsed and they plummeted into pitch darkness.

Penny curled protectively over Volantino as she plummeted down the slippery underground pipe. Bonvoyage gripped her satchel strap in both paws, whimpering as they swerved left, then right, then left again. Penny scrunched her eyes shut, hearing Volantino's feathers ruffling in the rush of air, and feeling his warm wings under her hands. Finally, she sensed herself slowing, and the tunnel dropping less steeply. She held her breath and gathered her nerves …

She fell through thin air and landed with a *flump* on to a soft pile of squashy mail sacks. There were two smaller bumps beside her as Wishyouwas and Cartolina landed and rolled over. She fished the torch from inside her satchel and clicked it on.

'*Fantastico!*' exclaimed Cartolina, shaking out her fur and pushing her glasses back up her nose. She blinked up at the high, hollow chamber, pocked with holes, that led to all the postboxes in London.

Bonvoyage, however, trembled as he slithered off the mound and on to the floor. His fur was pale, with a mouldy-green tinge.

'Are you all right?' Penny asked.

'*Oui, m-merci!*' Bonvoyage stumbled and weaved in a wobbly line. 'B-Bonvoyage is afraid of n-nothing!'

'Except heights,' Cartolina whispered behind her paw.

'We has to go this way.' Wishyouwas scampered up to one of several arched openings that encircled the chamber. This time it felt familiar to Penny, and she didn't hesitate to follow his pattering paws in the thin beam of her torch. Before long they branched on to the shinier tracks of the post office underground railway. They stayed quiet, and when the rattling squeal of a train approached, flattened themselves against the wall as it tore past them, towards Mount Pleasant.

They reached the fork in the tunnel. Penny breathed out a sigh when at last the Front Gate gleamed in the light of her torch.

Wishyouwas jabbed the button on the speaker and said their names. Moments later the gate swung inwards, flooding the tunnel with light. Penny squinted in the sudden brightness, and then blinked at the odd sight before them.

Private and Confidential looked as if they were going detecting in Antarctica. Their bodies were wrapped in mackintoshes, their heads were adorned with woolly hats made from human gloves with the fingers chopped off, and they both carried umbrellas fashioned from pens glued to corrugated biscuit tin lids. Behind them, a line of Sorters struggled to carry an array of implements including binoculars, magnifying glasses, pencil cases, balls of string and rolled-up maps.

'Where are you all going?' asked Penny.

'To locate the DLB and then find the Monarch's Seal, of course!' said Confidential. 'The question we might ask is where have *you* been? Their Highnesses expressly told you to stay inside the Bureau.'

Bonvoyage let out a snort. 'I do not understand your language,' he said with a shrug. 'Inside, outside, what difference does it make?'

'All the difference!' snapped Private.

'What matters is what we found,' Penny said. 'We came back to show you.' She rested Volantino on the ground, then opened her satchel, pulled the waxcloth package out and passed it to Wishyouwas.

Private and Confidential eyed it closely as he unwrapped it.

'The – the Monarch's Seal!' spluttered Private. He glared at Wishyouwas. 'Where did you gather this?'

Wishyouwas told them about the trail of clues from the DLB to the Abbey. Just before he got to the part about the envelope not smelling old enough, Confidential interrupted.

'And now you have come back to steal our thunder.'

Bonvoyage tilted his head at the ceiling. 'You 'ear thunder in the tunnels?'

'Stop annoying them,' Cartolina hissed, nudging him. 'We need their help.'

'You are not leading this case!' snapped Private, who had turned the shade of dark oak. 'It was *our* initial intelligence that led to the DLB. Therefore, *we* shall present the Monarch's Seal to Their Highnesses.'

Confidential jutted out a paw. 'If you please,' she said.

Penny shook her head. 'No, it's better if we take it. There's something odd about the letter. It might not be—'

'You may have done the gathering,' Private cut in, 'kindly let SWALK do the solving.' He whisked the envelope out of Wishyouwas's paw. 'We shall present this at the twelve o'clock Audience.' As they turned, the other Sorters twittered excitedly at the sight of the letter, and Private and Confidential walked between them like conquering heroes.

'Nincompoops,' said Bonvoyage. 'They think they 'ave solved the 'ole case!'

'And what if it *isn't* the real letter?' Penny said.

Wishyouwas lifted his chin. 'We just has to try and find out ourselves,' he squeaked. 'That is what Thiswayup would have done.'

'Thiswayup ...' Penny echoed, as an idea sparked in her mind. 'I think I know how we can solve it!'

14

Suspended From Duty

'A fter the Audience, we need to try and get the letter away from Private and Confidential for a few minutes,' Penny whispered.

Wishyouwas, Cartolina, Bonvoyage and Volantino leaned closer to her, their heads almost touching as they formed a tight circle behind a stack of parcel boxes, so that the other Sorters didn't overhear their Secret Society of Very Important Post meeting.

'Once we have the letter,' she continued, 'we can use the Automatic Letter Opener to steam it open without damaging it.'

'But only the Royal Postmistress is allowed to read it,' Wishyouwas squeaked.

Penny grinned. 'We don't need to read it. Lady Vellum told us that the letter is written on Italian papyrus. Cartolina, do you think you could smell if it was the right paper, if we open just a corner of the envelope?'

Cartolina's eyes gleamed, and she nodded. '*Si!* In Italy, papyrus was used for writing letters in ancient times. We learn about this as young Sorters. I will know its smell at once.'

Bonvoyage grimaced. 'But 'ow can we sneak the letter away from the nincompoops?'

Already the bossy tones of Stampduty announcing the twelve o'clock Audience drifted towards them from the far end of the tunnel. After that came a flurry of clapping paws and Penny guessed Private and Confidential had just presented the letter.

'We will need a distraction,' said Cartolina.

All four of them looked at Volantino. The pigeon cooed happily and dipped his head.

'*Voilà!* Then the plan is all wrapped up,' said Bonvoyage. 'Easy-cheesy.'

They had just jumped to their feet and paws when, from the direction of the Front Gate, the air shuddered with a booming voice that sounded like it was coming through a station loudspeaker. 'TAKE ME TO THE SORTERS IN CHARGE!'

Penny froze and the Sorters tensed, their tails flicking. An earthquake seemed to shake the tunnel as footsteps thudded towards them. *I know that voice!* Penny thought, and shared a startled look with Wishyouwas, whose ears twitched in alarm.

Moments later the Court Postmaster rounded the corner and stormed towards them like a human thundercloud, stooping to avoid hitting his head on the tunnel roof. He was followed by at least a dozen men and women in Royal Mail uniforms, holding fistfuls of empty mail sacks. They stared around them at the Sorters' buildings and equipment with wide-eyed astonishment.

'This is the Lost Letter Bureau!' barked Fragile,

scampering to keep up with the Court Postmaster's long strides, his hat askew. 'You can't just barge in during an Audience!'

'Sorters are in charge here,' added Handlewithcare. 'Not humans.'

'I am the Court Postmaster, and I carry the direct authority of Her Majesty the Queen when it comes to postal matters,' Mr Quilling bellowed, his voice amplified by the tunnel. Penny's mind whirled. He had been cross with her and Wishyouwas at the palace, but now he seemed furious. Was it because they had found the Monarch's Seal, after he expressly asked them not to? But then, how would he even know?

'Mr Quilling,' she said, standing in his path. Wishyouwas leaped to her shoulder.

'You two again!' He stopped and glared his blazing brown eyes at them. 'Did you have anything to do with this?'

Penny frowned. 'To do with what?'

'That is what I am here to find out.' He carried on, thumping past them, and Penny hurried behind him with Wishyouwas, Cartolina and Bonvoyage scampering at her heels.

They reached the letterbox avenue where the Audience had gathered. Sorters scattered out of Mr Quilling's way like tenpins knocked sideways by a bowling ball a hundred times their size. He seemed to fill the entire tunnel.

The Monarch's Seal had been propped up on the platform in front of the postbox, its red wax seal in full view. Private and Confidential stood on each side of it. The platform of Post Office Directories shook at each of Mr Quilling's steps.

He stopped, leaned down, and for a moment Penny thought he was bowing to Dearsir and Dearmadam. But then he roared, 'The Monarch's Seal, in your very paws!'

Even though he dwarfed them, Their Highnesses sat proudly upright on their inkwell thrones. 'Indeed, our Solvers were just telling us about the parcel of trouble they went to in order to retrieve it,' said Dearmadam. Private and Confidential's fur flushed reddish brown.

Mr Quilling shook his head and began pacing in front of their postbox. 'Despite the fact you have access to the Special Branch, and know how to pick locks, I never believed the Sorters were capable of such a deed. Not as fellow members of the Royal Mail. That is why I warned your envoys to have nothing to do with the missing Monarch's Seal in the first place.' His eyes snapped to Penny and Wishyouwas.

Dearsir and Dearmadam plumped up their fur. 'The Sorters are capable of a great many deeds,' Dearsir said with a tilt of his chin. 'Including this one.'

If possible, Mr Quilling looked even angrier, Penny thought. His moustache seemed to bristle. Then her eyes fell to the platform and she swallowed. Like invisible ink held up to a lightbulb, the picture Mr Quilling could see suddenly became clear.

He tugged a folded piece of paper out of his waistcoat pocket. 'An hour ago, I received an anonymous message. It says that the Monarch's Seal was stolen by the Sorters and is likely hidden in the Lost Letter Bureau.'

A shockwave rippled over the Sorters. The awful accusation hit Penny in the chest like a blow.

'How can you accuse us of this terrible crime?' croaked Dearsir. 'We are loyal to the Royal Postmistress!'

Wishyouwas stamped his paw. 'We never stole nothing. We finded the letter.'

'Then explain why you have the Monarch's Seal right here, plain as day.'

'It wasn't the Sorters,' Penny said breathlessly. 'They're innocent. We found the letter at the Abbey after following a trail of clues.'

Mr Quilling hooked his thumbs in his waistcoat pockets. 'Show me the clues,' he said.

Penny opened and shut her mouth. Wishyouwas's fur paled. 'We lefted them where they was,' he said. 'But we writed down copies.'

Bonvoyage had already dived into Penny's satchel. He poked his head out and held up his notepad. 'I 'ave them 'ere!'

'How do I know you haven't written some nonsense to cover your tracks?'

Penny had a sudden suspicion. 'Mr Quilling, may I see the message you received?'

'Very well,' he grunted, and unfolded the paper.

Penny's ribs drew in tight, as if a rubber band were wrapped around her. The words on the message had been cut out of different snippets of handwriting, just like the clues.

'Someone *was* spying on us,' she said. 'We thought we were ahead of them, but we were behind them all along. It must be the spy who sent you the message, after they saw us find the letter.' She glanced down at the envelope, even surer now that it couldn't be real. 'Maybe, to hide the real Monarch's Seal's location, they left this copy knowing we would find it?'

'A counterfeit?' Mr Quilling's chest swelled at an alarming rate. He snatched up the Monarch's Seal, turned it over and flinched. He whipped a letter opener from his waistcoat pocket and sliced the envelope open with a sharp *rrrrip!* that was quickly drowned out by the Sorters' giant, collective gasp of shock.

Mr Quilling unfolded the letter and held it up for them all to see. The paper was completely blank. 'As you will know, all letters are franked with a date and postmark before delivery, even the Monarch's Seal. I franked it myself at the Court Post Office just before locking it in the Red Box. The counterfeiter obviously forgot that. Or they didn't see it. Because *this* letter isn't franked. I now know why the key to my secure cabinet went missing. It is where the royal letter paper and wax seals are kept. Someone crept into my office and stole it, right under my nose.'

Penny's heart hammered. 'So the Monarch's Seal is still out there somewhere.'

'Out there?' replied Mr Quilling, bunching his bushy eyebrows. 'Or *in here*?' His eyes flashed. 'For all I know, you might have been stealing Her Majesty's mail for months, using the Special Branch.'

'It wasn't the Sorters!' Penny insisted, clenching her fists.

'Sorters never steal!' cried a chorus of voices.

'That is what I would rather believe,' Mr Quilling said. A heavy sigh escaped him. 'But the coronation is only hours away, and the Monarch's Seal *must* be found. I have no choice but to investigate every possibility, however difficult.' He turned and faced Their Highnesses, casting a shadow over them.

Cold dread crept through Penny's bones. Wishyouwas's paws curled on her shoulder.

'In the name of Her Majesty Queen Elizabeth, I hereby suspend your royal warrant as Guardians of Lost Letters, until further notice,' Mr Quilling said.

'S-suspended?' stuttered Dearsir.

'None of you are to leave the Bureau until it has been thoroughly searched.' Mr Quilling turned to the line of postmen and postwomen behind him, and nodded.

They dispersed along the tunnel. The Audience broke apart as Penny and the Sorters ran to follow them.

The posties began yanking drawers out of cupboards, sweeping contents off shelves and lifting the lids on desks, before rummaging around inside them and stuffing any letters they found inside the mail sacks.

Penny's breath rushed out of her. 'What are you doing?' she asked a postwoman, who looked up and accidentally dropped an envelope. A young Solver darted forwards and scooped it up, clinging on tightly as the postwoman tried to shake her loose.

'You cannot take it, this letter hasn't been solved yet!' she squeaked.

'I'm sorry. Our orders are to seize all the lost letters. We're taking them to the palace to search for the Monarch's Seal and any other royal letters,' the postwoman explained.

The Solver let go with a sob. Penny spun round. The tunnel filled with the chaotic sounds of crashing, clattering and rustling. The Sorters stood around in scattered huddles, looking tiny and helpless next to the big, clumping boots of the humans. Overturned parcel boxes soon lay everywhere, and the trundling conveyor belt had been stripped of letters. Filing cabinets stood open like sets of steps, their insides scooped out. Even the Sorters' letterbox homes had been opened and searched. Wishyouwas leaped to the ground and scurried up to letterbox number *16*, but Penny's letters had already been peeled off the walls. His whiskers drooped.

The Bureau was being tipped upside down and inside out. Everything the Sorters held most dear was being taken away, but worst of all – they were no longer trusted. And Penny knew, she was *certain*, that it was all for nothing. The Monarch's Seal would never be found among the lost letters.

Wishyouwas must have felt the same, because his whole body hunched over. 'I has failed the Royal Postmistress.'

Cartolina hopped into his letterbox and Volantino landed on top, ruffling his feathers.

Bonvoyage joined them and wrapped an arm around Wishyouwas's shoulder. For once, his face was long and serious. 'This is like *papier mâché* – a big mess!'

'How can we prove we are innocent?' Cartolina asked.

They looked at each other with blank faces. 'I don't think we can,' Penny said. 'Nobody else except Lady Vellum knows about the mission …' She gasped. 'That's it! Lady Vellum is even more important than Mr Quilling. If we tell her what's going on, she can get this stopped.'

'That is a good idea, but we cannot leave the Bureau,' Cartolina pointed out. 'I ran to the Front Gate. The humans are there, carrying out sacks and loading them on to a train.'

Wishyouwas's ears perked up a little. 'If we sneaks out, we can ride on the train too.'

Penny chewed her lip. 'You're all small enough to hide on the train, but they'll see me. Then we'll look even more guilty.'

'I know how we is getting you out without nobody seeing,' Wishyouwas said, hopping to the ground. 'We just has to find a sack.' He beckoned them to follow.

Penny crept along the edges of the tunnel behind him, towards the Front Gate. She kept looking over her shoulder, her heart heavy. The Bureau was almost emptied of lost letters. Solvers milled around with nothing to gather, solve or deliver. Almost no scrap of paper was left behind.

Close to the Sorters' telephone booth, they found an empty mail sack on the ground, dropped by the posties. Wishyouwas darted forwards and, together with Bonvoyage and Cartolina, dragged it to the side of the tunnel. He swivelled his head left and right. 'Dear Penny, climb in quick!' he squeaked. 'I is getting in with you.'

Penny also checked nobody was watching before wriggling into the sack, with Wishyouwas perching on her shoulder. Cartolina climbed up and tied it at the top.

'We will hide and open it at the other end,' she murmured through the sackcloth.

Penny hugged her knees, holding her breath. Then she heard thudding footsteps and was hoisted into the air.

'Crikey!' wheezed a postman's voice from above. 'This one's heavy.'

Penny bumped against his back, before everything went dark and she landed on something soft and crackly, which she guessed was other sacks of mail. She tried not to move a muscle, except for her finger, which she curled around Wishyouwas's paw. Together, they held on tight.

Wings and Claws

15

Wings and Claws

The Special Branch train jolted and rolled forwards. Wishyouwas wrapped his tail around Penny's neck as they hunched inside the sack.

With a screech of metal, the engine picked up speed and rattled over the rails. Penny bumped and juddered. Her tummy clenched queasily by the time the engine finally gave a long, loud hiss and slowed to a stop. After that, she couldn't hear anything. She didn't dare move until she knew it was safe.

Wishyouwas nibbled a hole in the sack, wriggled and peeped out, then ducked back in again. 'Dear

Penny!' he squeaked in warning, but the sack had already been untied and fell off her shoulders.

'Your letters or your life!' shouted Spam, wielding a broom in the air like a sword. Her tangle of frizzy hair made her look wild.

Penny froze solid. How could they have forgotten about her? Now they were caught and Mr Quilling would be *convinced* they were guilty. She glanced sideways – maybe Wishyouwas and the others could still make a run for it?

Spam's oversized eyes blinked behind her glasses and she set the broom down with a sigh. 'I thought that line was quite good. It's not much fun down here on my own. Nice to see you again.' She offered Penny her hand.

'Wh-what?' Penny stammered, holding her hand and scrambling off the sacks. 'Aren't you going to ask why we're here?'

Bonvoyage, Cartolina and Volantino had begun to emerge from among the sacks but ducked out of sight again as Spam threw back her head and guffawed. 'Ooh hoo! As if I don't know everything that happens on the Special Branch. You've escaped to try and clear your good names, haven't you? Old Quilling needs his bloomin' eyes checked, if you ask me. I told him when he got on the train to go to the Bureau, I said, "Nothing gets past the Special Branch without *me* seeing."' Spam tapped her glasses. 'And the first time I ever saw a Sorter was yesterday, when I met you. No.' She sniffed, her face suddenly serious. 'This nasty business with the Monarch's Seal has the smell of human, not Sorter.'

'So you believe we is innocent?' Wishyouwas asked.

'I do.' Spam stood up straight. 'You may pass,' she said with a grand sweep of her broom. 'I'll delay the train going back for Quilling and the others, to buy you some time. Spam's got your back, don't worry about that. And as for the lost letters, they'll be safe with me for now.'

'Thank you!' Penny and Wishyouwas said at the same time.

'*Grazie!*' Cartolina bowed her head. She hopped on to the platform with Volantino.

Bonvoyage jumped on to Spam's arm and kissed her hand, making her blush. She ushered them over the platform and opened the door for them on to the steep staircase. 'There's a button at the top of the stairs to open the map wall,' she said.

The Sorters formed a line and scurried up the stairs with Wishyouwas at the front and Volantino flying over their heads. But before Penny went up, Spam gently tugged her arm and her eyes sparkled, almost like a Sorter herself. 'There's something very wrong at the palace,' she whispered. 'If old Quilling's got the wrong end of the stick, it means you're our last hope of finding the Monarch's Seal and catching whoever stole it. I hope you do, for all our sakes!' Then she closed the door and plunged them into darkness.

Penny dug her torch from her satchel and clicked it on before climbing the staircase. The Sorters had already found the button and the map wall swung open with a soft creak, on to the dark, empty Court Post Office. Penny slid the torchlight over the counter, cabinets and shelves, feeling horribly like a thief. They all jumped as a clock chimed one in the morning.

Reaching the window, Penny lifted the corner of a blind to reveal the village-like courtyard of buildings and shops below them. The rain coated everything with an oily sheen. Her eyes travelled to Lady Vellum's house directly opposite, and her heart leaped. The lights were on in the topmost room! Then she jumped back as the black busby hat of a royal guard bobbed on patrol close by.

'We have to get across,' she whispered. She gave Wishyouwas the paperclip from her pendant again and he unlocked the post office door.

'I will listen for when the coast is clear,' Cartolina said. She dangled from the handle and put her ear against the keyhole. Her tail twitched like an antenna. Penny tensed.

'Now, *Cara Penny!*'

Penny opened the door and flew across the rain-swept courtyard, crouching low and trying not to splash through the puddles. Wishyouwas scampered ahead at full speed, and already had Lady Vellum's house unlocked before she got there. Penny burst through the door, dripping and panting.

The Sorters scurried through it after her.

'You will be safe outside, Volantino. We will be back soon,' said Cartolina, and the pigeon dipped his head.

They closed the door softly, then moved silently along the grey carpeted corridor and up the winding staircase.

Penny stopped outside Lady Vellum's office on

the top floor, giddy with relief. They had done it! Wishyouwas shook the raindrops off his fur, filled his body with air, and knocked.

They waited, but nobody answered.

Penny knocked even louder, and Lady Vellum still didn't answer. 'The lights were on though,' she said. With no other option she tried the handle. The door opened wide.

A chill gust of wind whipped Penny's hair around her face. The window was half open and a bright lamp was on, giving the grey room a cold glow. But nobody sat at the desk. The office was empty.

'Oh, no!' Penny's shoulders sank.

'Maybe she will come back. Let us go inside and wait,' suggested Cartolina. 'After all, we cannot return to the Bureau.'

Penny edged inside. *Doesn't Lady Vellum get cold?* she wondered, remembering she hadn't worn a coat at Westminster Abbey, despite the storm.

She sat on the floor next to the desk. The damp breeze crept beneath her coat and made her shiver.

The Sorters puffed out their fur and huddled close to her.

'*Brrr*, this British weather!' complained Bonvoyage. 'Now it is snowing, even in June!' He stooped and picked up a small, white fleck of something from the floor.

Cartolina sniffed it. 'That is paper, not snow,' she said.

Penny saw another white fragment lying close to the wastepaper basket. 'They've been blown out by the wind,' she said. She picked it up.

'Look, look!' Bonvoyage suddenly jumped up and pointed at it. 'There is writing!'

Penny turned the paper over. Written in black ink was the word:

Find

Bonvoyage laid his own fragment on the floor. In a different style of handwriting, this one read:

nection

'The pieces look like they was cutted out of letters,' Wishyouwas said. 'Just like the clues we finded.' He widened his eyes at Penny, and a prickling unease began to creep over her skin.

'It could be a coincidence,' Penny said. 'Lady Vellum hates making mistakes. Maybe she just cut these bits out of a letter.' But that didn't make sense because the handwritings were *different*. Something else tugged at her mind. 'Bonvoyage, do you still have your copies of the clues?'

'Of course!' He opened her satchel and scrambled inside it, before reappearing with his notepad. He licked a finger and riffled through to the right page.

Penny read the first clue, '*hint on tree*'. She looked back at the paper fragments and tried to combine the bits of words together in her head to see if they made a whole new word, but nothing worked. Then she read the second clue. '*A b fal con.*' She glanced at the paper fragments again and let out a sharp gasp. 'If you put *con* and *nection* together, it makes *connection*!'

'Hmm,' Cartolina said thoughtfully. 'But without the original clues, we cannot see if the handwriting matches.'

'I will find more!' Bonvoyage said. He dived off the desk into the wastepaper basket as if it were a swimming pool. Scrunched-up papers jumped out of it like popcorn. Penny and the others flattened them all out on the floor. Some were half-finished letters with ink spots on them, but they found several which had small segments missing, where words had been neatly snipped out with scissors. Penny's gaze caught on one of them:

May it please Your Majesty,

In honour of your coronation, we have planted a new   in the children's park at Coram's Fields.

The room suddenly felt much, much colder. 'The word "tree" is missing,' she whispered. 'But if it *was* Lady Vellum who made the clues we found, that means ...'

'She also maked the pretend Monarch's Seal, which gotted us into trouble,' Wishyouwas finished, his tail flicking side to side.

Penny sucked in a breath. 'Then it was Lady Vellum who took the key to Mr Quilling's cabinet. But why would she do all of that, just to make us find the wrong letter?'

Bonvoyage spun his cap on his finger. 'Per'aps she stole the real one.' He glanced at them all. 'What is wrong? You look like fish!'

Penny, Cartolina and Wishyouwas all had their mouths open. It was a serious accusation and, coming so soon after the Sorters had been wrongly accused, Penny couldn't let herself believe it. Neither, it seemed, could Wishyouwas.

'Her duty is to the Royal Postmistress,' he squeaked.

'And I don't see how,' Penny added. 'Lady Vellum was at the Court Post Office before the Monarch's Seal even got delivered. It would have been impossible to steal it then without anybody seeing, wouldn't it?'

A sudden scuffle sounded from the window and Volantino landed on the sill. He flapped his wings and let out a short, sharp coo.

'He is warning us!' Cartolina said.

Bonvoyage bounded over to the door and listened, then made quick flapping motions with his paws and ran a long finger across his neck.

Lady Vellum was coming back! A lightning bolt of panic shot up Penny's spine. She scrambled to sweep up the scattered papers into the bin with Wishyouwas and Cartolina's help, just as the door handle began to turn.

16

Two Birds with One Stone

As the door handle lowered, Penny's limbs locked. Only minutes ago they had wanted Lady Vellum's help. Now she might be the thief!

'Psst, hide!' Bonvoyage urged her.

There was only one place *to* hide. Penny forced herself to dive into the alcove beneath Lady Vellum's desk, pulling her satchel behind her. She curled into a tight ball and the Sorters crouched close.

Volantino cooed loudly as the door opened.

'Ugh. I thought I heard a sound,' Lady Vellum said. 'Nasty, filthy pigeon!'

Penny flinched at the coldness of her tone. From beneath the desk she could just see the points of Lady Vellum's pencil-thin stilettos stab the carpet as she strode quickly across the room. Her heart thumped with every step.

Lady Vellum skirted around the desk and her feather boa slipped to the floor, landing in a feathery heap.

'Shoo, you stupid bird!' she cried.

Volantino flapped his wings and launched off the sill. He flew in wide circles around her office and landed on top of the hatstand.

'Calamus will crunch your bones for his breakfast!' Lady Vellum hissed.

There was no trace of kindness in her voice now, and Penny's doubts about the Royal Secretary grew. She held her breath as the desk drawer slid open above her head. Lady Vellum took something out and closed it again. After that Penny caught the *swish* of the window sash being lifted higher and the breeze in the room grew stronger. Lady Vellum whistled a wavering note into the night.

Volantino landed on the floor and waddled into Penny's open satchel. The Sorters waited in a tense row, their back paws digging into the carpet and preparing to spring for the door. Wishyouwas's moonlike eyes were locked on Penny's.

Suddenly a heavy beat of wings came from the window. Penny couldn't see what had made the noise but Wishyouwas, Cartolina and Bonvoyage's tails went ramrod straight and their fur stood up, each hair quivering. Penny had never seen Sorters show such fear. Her own skin felt as if frosty fingers were running over it.

Trying not to make a sound, or even breathe, Penny inched her head from under the desk until she could glimpse the window. She gulped down a gasp.

A huge falcon landed upon the sill, shaking raindrops off its mottled, grey-and-white wing feathers. It was easily five times the size of a Sorter, with dripping yellow talons like blades. Lady Vellum

chium ... ... put the
trail. She had ... ... sure they
round the counterfeit letter. And she must have sent

wore a long leather glove over one arm, which she must have taken from the drawer. The bird hopped on to her clenched fist, and Penny noticed a metal canister attached by a leather cord around one of its legs.

'Dear Calamus,' said Lady Vellum with a toothy hiss. 'I have a fresh snack for you.' The bird gave a feathery rustle in reply. Lady Vellum's high heels swivelled round. 'Where has it gone?' she snapped. 'Where is that dratted pigeon?'

The falcon opened its beak and made a rasping, *kak-kak-kak* sound.

'Shh,' soothed Lady Vellum. 'Never mind, my

sweet. Tomorrow I will bring you a live mouse or rat from the traps in the cellar. Perhaps a whole cageful. Because we have won! The Sorters took the bait, and that fool Quilling believed everything. They are finished, and we are free. Ha ha!'

Penny's blood seemed to stop flowing. Lady Vellum had betrayed them all! *She* had laid the trail. *She* had followed them to make sure they found the counterfeit letter. And *she* must have sent the anonymous note to Mr Quilling, saying the Sorters had stolen the Monarch's Seal …

It's my fault! she thought with a stab of icy guilt. She had been so determined to help Wishyouwas solve the clues, to help him before she left London, that she had helped him and all the Sorters fall straight into a trap.

Lady Vellum's heels spun round towards the window. 'There is just one more little job you must do for me before I give you your reward,' she said to Calamus. 'We must hide anything that could implicate *us* in the theft of the Monarch's Seal.'

Penny didn't see what happened next, but she heard a metallic twisting sound.

'Ouch!' Lady Vellum cried. 'Naughty Calamus! I know you do not like wearing the canister but you must keep hold of this letter for me, to stop it being found before tomorrow.' The scraping sounded again. 'There. We wouldn't want everything to unravel at the last moment, would we? Then we can sell the Monarch's Seal to the highest bidder, safe in the knowledge we shall never be caught. We shall kill two birds with one stone, ha ha!'

Penny stifled a gasp. Bonvoyage was right. Lady Vellum *was* the thief! And she had just given a letter to Calamus …

'The Monarch's Seal!' she mouthed to Wishyouwas, and he nodded back. His paws were bunched so tight his knuckles were white. But the falcon would rip them all to shreds if they tried to get near it. There was nothing they could do except cower beneath the desk and wait.

Then it was too late. With a piercing cry, Calamus spread his wings as wide as the window. They beat up and down, making the curtains billow, and then the bird of prey launched into the night sky. Wishyouwas sank down, his ears flat with defeat.

Lady Vellum slid the window shut, replaced her glove in the desk drawer, and then crossed the room, snapping the light off and shutting the door. The *tap-tap* of her heels faded.

Penny let out a huge, shaky breath. 'We have to get back to Spam and tell her about Lady Vellum,' she said to the others. 'She's the only one who might believe us.'

They scrambled out from under the desk and out of the office. Wishyouwas rode the banister down, but then he suddenly twisted round and scrambled back up again. 'She is coming back!' he squeaked.

'What?' Penny gasped. She turned and climbed, but already she could hear Lady Vellum's sharp heels tapping up the flight below, getting louder and closer. They would be seen before they could hide again in her office!

'*Psst!*' Bonvoyage whispered, pointing at the huge grandfather clock on the landing. 'In 'ere!' Penny opened the glass front and they all climbed inside. She felt the pendulum swishing just behind her back and her heart thrummed like a humming-bird's wings. Through the glass she saw Lady Vellum's brown curls appear, and tensed. Surely she would see her!

But, to her amazement, Lady Vellum walked right past without giving a single glance to the clock. 'I must find my feather boa,' she muttered, holding a hand to her neck. She entered her office.

In a heartbeat Penny was out of the clock and half running, half sliding down the stairs, the Sorters leaping four steps at a time beside her. At the bottom they fled along the corridor and burst outside, running before they had even looked.

Penny was halfway across the courtyard when she heard a man yell and boots chop over the wet cobbles. She sprinted forward, desperate to make it to the Special Branch in time – but she didn't even have time to reach Wishyouwas, his eyes wide with fear as he waited for her outside the Court Post Office. He stretched his paw towards her – before a heavy hand landed on her shoulder.

Mischev

17

Mayday

'Please,' Penny pleaded. 'Let me go. There's a thief in the palace. I need to speak to—'

'There's a thief, all right,' the royal guard said, cutting her off. He loomed over her, enormously tall and fierce in his busby hat. 'You're the kid from earlier who wanted to see Lady Vellum. I wondered why we didn't see you leave the palace. Hid somewhere to wait until dark, did you? Thought you'd try and steal some treasures?'

'No!' Penny cried.

'This time it's the guardroom for you. I'll

telephone the police and you can explain everything to them. You're in a lot of trouble, young lady.' He marched her over the cobbles, away from the post office.

Telephone … trouble … Penny remembered something. She slid her hand in her coat pocket and felt a small, hard wrapper. Unravelling the scrap of paper, she curled her hand over the penny coin Thiswayup had left for her.

'Can I please telephone my mother?' she asked. 'She doesn't know where I am and will be so worried if I don't come home.'

The guard hesitated. 'I'll have to listen,' he said. 'You're *only* to tell her where you are. Nothing else. Otherwise you might be passing instructions to fellow thieves.'

Penny's cheeks flushed but she nodded, her mind racing. She hurried to the telephone box outside the post office, and the soldier wedged the door open with his boot. He turned his face away but would be able to hear every word she said.

Through the glass panes of the booth, Penny saw a small furry face peer at her with wide, worried eyes. She crossed her fingers and dropped the penny into the coin slot. Carefully she dialled the number for Uncle Frank's post office: POST-1516. The line on the end of the receiver whirred as it connected.

Seconds later, her mother's warm burr came through clearly at the other end. 'Hello?'

Penny's eyes welled up. 'Mum, it's me,' she said. 'I'm sorry to call you on a ... May day.' She glanced at the guard, but he didn't turn round.

There was a pause. 'I can't hear you well,' her mother said. 'Please repeat, much more slowly. And tell me, where are you calling from?'

Penny swallowed. 'I said, sorry to call you on a May day. I'm at Buckingham Palace. I wish you was here.'

'That'll do,' said the guard.

Penny hooked the receiver and bit her lip, hoping her secret message had got through.

'You got the month wrong,' the guard said as she left the telephone box. 'It's the second of June today.'

'Oh, really?' Penny said, hoping he didn't mention it further. She knew pilots said 'Mayday' in an emergency. Her mum had told her it came from the French word *m'aidez*, which means 'help me'. She glanced over her shoulder and thought she saw three small shadows flash along the edge of the courtyard.

They passed under the archway, and she saw the high black gates of the palace ahead with the angel statue beyond. There was no way out for her. She crossed her fingers that Wishyouwas would manage to get out and carry on –

'Oi! Excuse me!' a familiar voice shouted behind Penny. 'Wait up!'

The guard halted and swung round. Penny saw a bushy-haired wild woman running towards them holding a broom, and her heart skipped. Spam!

Spam, however, didn't even glance at Penny, as if she weren't there. She wore a brown coat over her station overalls and blinked at the guard, panting as she caught him up. 'Can you let me out of the palace, please?' she asked.

The guard stiffened. 'Who are you?'

Penny wondered why he didn't know, but then remembered Spam spent most of her time underground.

'I'm a cleaner,' Spam said, waving the broom in front of him. 'See? Had to work extra late cleaning the palace for the coronation. All sorts of important dignitaries are coming. And now I've missed the last bus home and I'll have to walk all the way. Ooh, my legs don't half ache,' she said, bending over and rubbing her knees. 'Do me a favour, and let me go quickly, won't you, please?' She glanced up and gave Penny a quick wink behind her glasses.

The guard frowned beneath his busby hat. 'Why have you brought your broom with you?' he challenged.

Spam didn't miss a beat. 'Doubles up as a walking stick,' she said.

The guard took a long breath. 'What a night,' he muttered. 'Very well.' He lifted a metal panel set into the stone of the archway and pressed a button inside it. The high black gates began to swing open.

'Thank you so much!' Spam said, and widened her eyes at Penny. 'Run!' she mouthed.

Suddenly Spam's broom swung through the air and the brush head knocked straight on top of the guard's furry black hat, pushing it down over his nose.

'Hey!' he roared, spinning in a circle while trying to wrench it off.

Penny sprinted for the gates, not daring to look back until she had passed the angel statue and was running full pelt along the soaking pavement. She could hear the Sorters at her heels as the four of them, now fugitives, raced away from the palace.

'We have to hide,' Penny panted.

'In here!' squeaked Wishyouwas, pointing to Penny's left.

St James's Park loomed beside them. It was so late that the lamp posts had been switched off. The black silhouettes of the trees looked spindly and sinister.

Wishyouwas scampered through the park gates, followed by Cartolina and Bonvoyage. Penny followed the sound of their paws on the rain-soaked path. She didn't dare click on her torch or even stop for breath until they reached the middle and darkest part of the park, beside the canal. At last, she leaned against the trunk of a willow tree, winded and wet through.

'Ha – we escaped,' gasped Bonvoyage, clutching his soggy paper hat against his heaving chest. 'It is a good thing we found the *magnifique* Spam.'

Cartolina's fur glistened, and her spectacles slid down her nose. 'But now we are on the run, and we still have no proof the Sorters are innocent of stealing.'

Wishyouwas's toes curled into the damp earth. 'And we hasn't got the lost letter for the Royal Postmistress,' he squeaked. He lifted his Deliverer's medallion, then let it fall with a bump beneath his chin.

Penny rubbed the tiredness from her eyes and paced under the willow branches to warm herself.

'Let's think. We know Lady Vellum gave the Monarch's Seal to Calamus. Where could the falcon have flown with it?'

Cartolina stroked the pigeon's head, and he let out an affectionate, warbling coo. 'Volantino always stays close to me. The falcon is trained, so he must also stay close to Lady Vellum. But falcons are not like pigeons. They like to be alone.'

'That means his roost must be somewhere close to the palace,' Penny said. 'But where?' She shivered and her thoughts began to feel sluggish. The Sorters were trembling too. She knew they all needed to find shelter soon, or they'd freeze. And it was too far to get to Uncle Frank's post office without a bicycle.

Then she remembered the abandoned bird-keeper's cottage they'd passed in the park yesterday. At least there they might be able to rest while they planned what to do next.

The Sorters' eyes shone like stars in the darkness as they set off along the lake shore. The reeds whispered and the slow lapping of the water sounded almost like footsteps, following them.

Finally, Wishyouwas stopped and pointed up at something poking between the trees – the crooked pillar of the cottage chimney. They pushed through the gap in the hedge and Penny's courage faltered. In the light, Duck Island Cottage had looked like something out of a fairytale. Now the building seemed strangely twisted out of shape, the plane tree crouching over it like a colossal spider. Moonlight reflected on the cracked windows, as if it were watching them.

Swallowing a lump of fear, Penny shone the torchlight over the ancient front door. She gave it a tentative push, and it swung open silently. *Someone has been here recently, or it would have made a sound*, she thought with a shiver of unease.

They edged inside in a huddle and Penny closed the door, shutting out most of the wind. There only seemed to be one room in the cottage. The boards gave ghostly creaks when Penny trod on them. A rickety, rotten bedframe stood close to an empty fireplace. A hollow loneliness filled the room, the same way her old bedroom had felt after her things had all been packed away. She rubbed her arms. 'If only we had some dry wood, we could make a fire,' she murmured.

Bonvoyage circled the room with his arms behind his back. '*Voilà!*' he cried, stopping and pointing above Penny's head. She shone her torch at the hole in the thatched roof, then beneath it saw a heap of fallen thatch, wedged between two rafters. She spotted a broom in a corner and used the bristly end to knock the heap to the floor. Sticks scattered everywhere, along with a pillow's worth of bird feathers.

'But how can we light it?' Penny said.

'Leave that to me.' Cartolina squatted and opened her spectacles case. Inside it was a folded-up wooden ruler, a thimble and a matchbox. 'I always travel prepared,' she said with a smile.

Bonvoyage rubbed his paws together. 'Soon this *petite maison* will be as warm as my 'eart!' Grabbing the matchbox and a pawful of dry sticks, he bounced over to the fireplace. In a few seconds he had a fire crackling to life, his eyes alight with devilish triumph.

Penny sank to the floor and hugged her knees in front of the glow, the Sorters curled up beside her. But the heat couldn't warm the deep-down coldness she had felt since leaving Buckingham Palace.

'Is you all right, Dear Penny?' Wishyouwas asked, leaping into her lap.

A lump rose in her throat. She had put off telling Wishyouwas for so long, and it had only heaped trouble upon him and all the Sorters. She knew the time had come to finally tell him, but she dreaded him being upset with her.

'I … I'm moving to Scotland as soon as the coronation is over,' she said in a small voice. A tear trickled down her cheek. 'I won't live in London any more and that means we won't be able to see each other. I've been wanting to tell you for ages, but I didn't know how. I'm so sorry for keeping it from you, Wishyouwas.' She held her breath.

Wishyouwas filled his cheeks with air, and then let it out in one long, slow puff. A tiny frown creased his face, but then he reached out and squeezed one of Penny's fingers. 'You doesn't have to be sorry, Dear Penny,' he said with a sad half-smile. 'I is glad you tolded me. We is always friends, no matter where you is.'

He leaped into her arms and clasped her neck. The cold seeped out of Penny's body as they hugged.

As the weight of worry she had carried for so long lifted, her body relaxed and her eyelids drooped. Even the nocturnal Sorters were nodding sleepily, and Volantino nestled his head under one wing. Penny knew they should be thinking of where they might find Calamus and the Monarch's Seal, but as she watched the dancing flames, smelt the soft, crackling woodsmoke and listened to the soothing sounds of the rain, her mind felt fuzzier than ever.

The time ticked past on Wishyouwas's medallion, and one by one they drifted into a doze.

Outside, the storm finally ran out of breath, and the sky beyond the window lightened. The darkest corners of the cottage turned a dull grey, then a fiery red, reflected from a warning sky.

18

Delivery Day

18

Delivery Day

'Dear Penny, wake up!'

Penny sensed something tugging her sleeve and cracked her eyes open. 'Wishyouwas?' she murmured, still half asleep.

'We has to go, Dear Penny!' He held her finger and tried to heave her up.

'What is it?' Penny asked, blinking blearily. Where was she? Then she remembered – the old cottage! What time was it? The fire had turned to ashes and pale sunlight seeped through the filthy windows. 'It's Coronation Day!' she gasped. 'Sorry I fell asleep. We've lost so much time …'

Then her breath caught.

Wishyouwas, Bonvoyage and Cartolina stood in a defensive line in front of her. Volantino poked his head out of her satchel, as if he were hiding from something.

Just then a piercing shriek came from the sky, making her hair crackle. Through the hole in the roof, in between the branches of the plane tree, she spotted a long-winged shape tilting and swerving on the air currents. She thought it was a gull at first, but as it hovered lower, growing larger, she saw its mottled grey underbelly, pointed wings and long, black-tipped tail.

'Calamus!' she gasped.

'It was his nest we destroyed,' said Cartolina. 'We must run now, while we can!'

Penny heaved to her feet, her muscles stiff as cardboard. She snatched up her satchel and stumbled for the door, just as a feathery arrow dropped through the hole in the roof and landed on the rafter. The falcon let out a cry that filled the whole cottage, and his wings beat like drums.

Penny startled and tripped over, rolling on to her back as she used her arms to protect Volantino inside her satchel.

The falcon peered down at her and the Sorters, his ringed yellow eyes glinting in the dim light. He scratched his talons against the rafter, revealing the small metal canister still strapped to his leg.

Wishyouwas's limbs were as tight as coiled springs, looking as if he were about to leap.

'No!' Cartolina laid a paw on his arm. 'You cannot get the letter. Peregrine falcons are the fastest animals alive. He will kill you while you are still in the air.'

'Then we make 'im come to the ground,' said Bonvoyage. He hopped forwards and shouted, 'Hey, nincompoop!'

'Bonvoyage, stop! What are you doing?' Cartolina hissed.

Calamus's head snapped round, blinking at Bonvoyage.

'You think you are so fast and clever?' the French

Sorter carried on, paws on hips. 'You could not catch a cold!'

The falcon stretched his wings. At full span they were enormous, dwarfing Cartolina's ruler.

Suddenly the falcon dived. Bonvoyage sprang forwards, aiming for the bird's leg, but Calamus was impossibly fast. He grabbed the Sorter in his talon and relaunched, soaring over their heads.

'Bonvoyage!' Penny cried, jumping for him. But it was hopeless. Calamus was well out of her reach, flapping between the rafters towards the hole in the roof.

''Elp!' Bonvoyage shrieked. His fur turned chalky pale, then he fell limp in a faint. His blue sailor hat fluttered to the ground.

Cartolina and Wishyouwas sprang through the air at the same time, higher than Penny had ever seen a Sorter jump. They landed on the rafter, and Wishyouwas wobbled to keep balance with only his half-tail.

Cartolina jumped between him and Calamus, spinning her wooden ruler like a propeller. As the falcon approached the hole, a sharp *thwack* on his talon sent him flapping sideways, but he didn't lose his grip on Bonvoyage. He landed on the rafter, only to receive another hard rap on the head. Cartolina ducked and dived as he jabbed at her with his razor-sharp beak.

Wishyouwas now joined Cartolina, swiping at the falcon's feathers with a twig. It was a feeble defence and the falcon struck like lightning. Wishyouwas almost lost an ear, darting backwards just in time.

Penny whirled, searching the cottage for anything she could use to help … The broom! She grabbed it and swung the bristly end at the falcon just as he lunged for Cartolina.

Calamus let out a piercing shriek and dropped Bonvoyage.

Penny caught his tiny, furry body in her arms, where he gave a strangled gasp.

Calamus flapped his wings in fury and clawed the roof, sending cobwebs and loose thatch tumbling down on to Wishyouwas and Cartolina's heads. As they curled up protectively, the falcon seized his chance and soared through the hole in the roof.

'Do not lose 'im … still a chance … find the Monarch's Seal …' Bonvoyage groaned. His fur was sickly green now, and his eyes rolled in his head.

With soft thuds, Wishyouwas and Cartolina dropped to the ground. Penny yanked the door open, and they ran out of the cottage into the park, hazy with morning drizzle.

Penny squinted, scanning the sky between the trees. 'There!' she said, pointing at a small, circling dark speck beneath the clouds. Calamus wheeled slowly eastwards, towards the rising sun and the River Thames.

She sprinted along the path. Wishyouwas and Cartolina hopped over the puddles, keeping pace, but as the park gates came into sight, Penny realised only Wishyouwas was by her feet, keeping his eyes locked on the sky.

Glancing backwards, she saw Cartolina hopping on her back paws, her forepaw clutched against her chest.

'Cartolina, you're hurt!' she cried, running back for her.

'*Si, Cara Penny*, but only a little,' she said, panting. 'The falcon was too fast for me.'

Penny picked her up and settled her in the satchel with Volantino and Bonvoyage. She looked back up, but Calamus had vanished from sight. Wishyouwas jumped on to her shoulder. 'If you run, Dear Penny, I is finding for the falcon,' he said, gripping on tight.

Outside the park, spectators had already begun gathering on the pavement, lining the route to Westminster Abbey to claim the best view of the coronation procession. They were hunkered beneath umbrellas cradling flasks of hot tea, and nobody gave Penny a glance as she rushed past. It felt agonisingly far and slow without the bicycle.

Wishyouwas pointed upwards. 'I sees the falcon!' he squeaked. Penny followed his paw. Calamus circled one of the high towers of Westminster Abbey, then veered away, towards the River Thames.

Penny pummelled her legs faster, following Wishyouwas's directions until she reached a low wall overlooking the river. A set of stone steps led down to a thin strip of strand lapped by steely waves. A small, abandoned-looking motorboat lay on its side close to the water's edge, but it may as well have been a dead end. Penny had no clue how to use it.

The falcon soared in effortless circles above the waves, as if he were taunting them.

Just then Penny's satchel opened, Volantino wriggled out and landed with a flutter on the river wall. He dipped his head to Wishyouwas, then wiggled his tail feathers.

Without hesitation Wishyouwas hopped on to Volantino's back. He wrapped both paws gently around the pigeon's chest, a determined grimace on his face. 'We isn't losing the letter again,' he said.

'No, wait, you'll be killed!' Penny cried. But already Volantino was beating his wings. With a hop and a jump the pigeon lifted into the air and flapped hard, with Wishyouwas's tail trailing like a short kite string behind him.

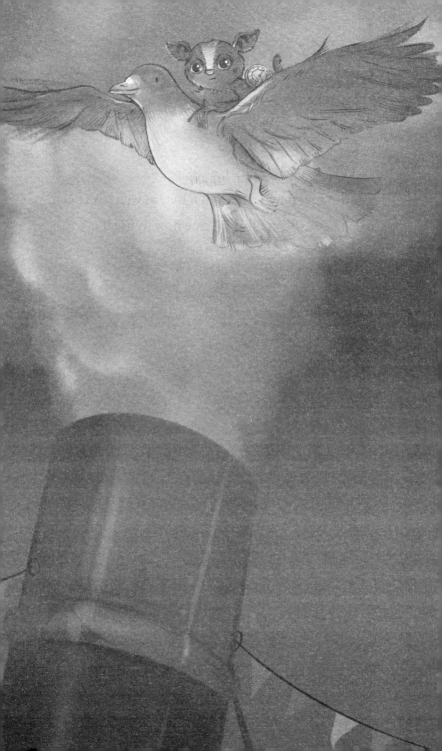

A steam packet was sailing along the river, smoke pouring from its chimney-like funnel. Volantino flew straight towards it, then began darting in and out of the smoke, using it as a screen to climb higher.

Penny looked up, and her heart lurched: Calamus lurked directly above the ship's funnel, also using the smoke to hover easily on its warm air currents. His head was lowered, his talons outstretched and waiting to pounce.

'Watch out!' she shouted, but her voice was snatched by the breeze.

Volantino sensed the danger. The pigeon flapped his wings, and shot away over the water. Calamus let out a shriek and swooped in a graceful arc, giving chase along the river.

'They'll never be able to outfly the falcon,' Penny said, her heart in her throat.

'Then we must sail!' Bonvoyage sprang out of her satchel on to the river wall, still a little wobbly. He gave a huge sniff, filling his lungs, and his fur began to return to its usual colour. '*Ahh, j'adore la mer*. Follow me, *mes amies!*'

Bonvoyage hopped down the steps and leaped aboard the motorboat. As soon as his paws touched the gunwale he perked up even more. He jumped on to the motor and wrapped the starter cable around his paw. Penny pushed it upright and gently rested Cartolina and her satchel on the bottom of the boat. Then she shoved with all her strength. It grated slowly, then slid towards the water and gathered speed on the slippery sand. Penny tumbled in just as it pushed off into the waves.

Vrooommmm! The engine whirred to life. Bonvoyage grabbed hold of the tiller, which looked enormous in his paws, and pushed the stick sideways, directing them upriver. The little boat bobbed over the waves, like a minnow among the whales of the enormous ships swiftly sailing by.

Penny gripped the prow, staring at the clouds. Then she saw Volantino and Wishyouwas, furiously flapping in their direction. Calamus streaked behind them, before folding his wings. With an extra burst of speed he shot past Volantino, who beat his feathers and changed direction mid-flight, now facing into the wind. It was a clever, deadly manoeuvre by the falcon.

With Wishyouwas on his back and the breeze against him, Penny could tell Volantino was swiftly tiring. He tried turning again and flew for the boat, losing height with every wingbeat. Calamus circled overhead, lowering and preparing to strike.

'They'll never reach us in time. We have to go faster!' Penny shouted.

'We are at full speed,' Bonvoyage called, steering the boat straight for them. The pigeon was now so low his body almost touched the waves. But he valiantly powered on, his grey head dipping in exhaustion. They were three boat-lengths away … now two …

Penny gasped out loud as suddenly the falcon dived like a silver bullet, his yellow talons outstretched towards the pigeon. Time seemed to slow, and in the same heartbeat she saw Wishyouwas leap high into the air, his long arms and legs at full stretch. He landed on the falcon's right wing, where he clung by one paw. Calamus screeched and pulled up, missing Volantino by a whisker. The falcon's long tail splashed the water, before taking off again. He tumbled through the air, stabbing at his own feathers to try and get at Wishyouwas. But Wishyouwas scrambled on to the falcon's back, where his deadly beak couldn't reach him, and clung on for his life.

Volantino landed on the bottom of the boat. Cartolina rushed over to him, while Penny kept her eyes strained on the sky until they ached, not even daring to blink her terrified tears away. She couldn't afford to lose sight of the falcon, even for a second.

She followed the swirling, winged shape against the clouds. Calamus was moving in odd jerks, which could only mean Wishyouwas was still riding him. Bonvoyage swung the tiller to the right, keeping the boat on the same course.

Calamus was turning somersaults in the sky to try and shake Wishyouwas off. Now the falcon was tiring. Unlike Volantino, the predator was clearly not used to having a rider on board, and he hated it. He flapped his wings in a storm of feathers, twisting in the air, but somehow Wishyouwas stayed on, a tiny brown speck against the bird's grey body. Penny craned her neck upwards, feeling sick with fear and filled with awe all at the same time. Now they were directly above the boat. Calamus beat his wings once, twice, and then the falcon seemed to stop in mid-air, as if frozen. And suddenly he dived down-wards, not flapping at all, just plummeting towards the river and showing no sign of stopping.

'They're going to hit the water!' Penny gasped, her voice a ragged shred. She saw Wishyouwas, his half-tail fluttering in the air as he desperately held on, paws wrapped tightly around the falcon's chest.

'It is only a trick,' said Cartolina. 'To make Wishyouwas fall off.'

True enough, at the last moment Calamus flung out his talons and tried to arch his wings, but Wishyouwas refused to let go and the falcon couldn't pull back up. With a *splash* they plunged into the river, sending up a high plume of water.

'Wishyouwas!' Penny screamed.

Bonvoyage stopped the engine and the boat

shuddered to a halt in midstream. Penny and the Sorters stared at the white-tipped waves.

Somewhere behind them Big Ben chimed eleven. Every *bong* of the massive bell felt endless to Penny. Then her heart leaped as, in a burst of spray, something shot back out of the water. But it was Calamus, only Calamus. The falcon spread his wings, his feathers pouring water, and fought the wind, climbing higher. The anklet and tether had come away from his leg and the falcon flew freely into the air, with a wild cry that carried far away on the wind. Within seconds he was nothing but a tiny speck in the sky.

Penny tore her eyes away and desperately searched the patch of bubbles on the water, but Wishyouwas did not appear. One by one the bubbles burst …

'*Excusez-moi!*' Bonvoyage cried. He swallow-dived off the prow of the boat into the water. Crawling on his front through the waves, he reached the last of the bubbles. As it popped, he took a deep gasp of air and plunged beneath the water.

Penny's chest grew tighter and tighter as they waited. The world around her faded, the wind and rain became nothing, and all that mattered was watching the water and clinging on to hope.

Bonvoyage's head suddenly broke the surface. 'Pah!' he spluttered, and sucked in a huge breath. He turned on to his back and paddled with his back paws, pulling a bedraggled brown bundle under one arm.

'He found him!' Penny leaned over the boat until she almost toppled in and pulled both of the cold, soggy Sorters out of the water, soaking her sleeves to the elbows. They lay in her arms, gasping and coughing up water while tears of relief ran down her face.

Wishyouwas stirred. He blinked at Penny, and his arm trembled as he lifted something up to show her: a small silver canister, tied to one end of leather cord. 'I gotted it back, Dear Penny,' he said in a weary whisper. But his mouth turned upwards in a smile and a gleam came into his moonlike eyes. 'I has the Monarch's Seal!'

19

Always on Time

Penny wormed her way along the packed streets towards Westminster Abbey, Bonvoyage and Wishyouwas scurrying at her heels. Wishyouwas wore the canister on his back, tied tightly around his middle with the leather cord to prevent it sliding off as he ducked in between the forest of legs.

By now the coronation had started. The royal procession was their last chance to reach the Queen before the ceremony, but getting the Monarch's Seal to her seemed impossible.

Union Jack flags waved above her head. The procession passed by with the *rat-a-tat-tat* of drums and the *clip-clop*, *clip-clop* of horses' hoofs. Red-coated royal guards lined the route, standing as still and straight as postboxes. Between them, she caught glimpses of coaches carrying lords and ladies, dukes and duchesses, and knew the Queen could not be far behind. An endless sea of people stood between her and the Abbey, and she tried to ignore the tuts and complaints as she pushed in, until she reached the barrier in front of the Abbey entrance.

Just in time.

A crescendo of cheers made the air shudder around her. Penny got goosebumps as a golden Cinderella coach led by eight white horses and flanked by footmen rolled slowly by. She leaned over the barrier and raised both her arms in the air, shouting, 'Here! Over here!'

From behind the coach window the Queen smiled and waved her hand. But she didn't seem to see Penny – or even Wishyouwas, who balanced on top of her head, waving both paws like mad. There were far too many flags and handkerchiefs fluttering in his way. Then it was too late. The coach moved on and he slid down to Penny's shoulder, his ears flat against his cheeks.

'It is 'opeless!' said Bonvoyage, who had clambered on to Penny's other shoulder. 'We will never be able to deliver the letter this way!'

Penny looked up at Westminster Abbey, so close but impossibly out of reach. Newspaper reporters and photographers surrounded the entrance. If only Volantino had been able to fly Wishyouwas over the crowds, she thought. But the poor pigeon was resting in her satchel with injured Cartolina, exhausted from his deadly race against the falcon.

She lowered her voice, even though the crowd was making more than enough noise to cover her. 'Let's see if there's another way in,' she suggested.

She backed out of the crowd and made for the rear of Westminster Abbey, where the tents and marquees still stood. There was no view of the procession from there, so there were hardly any

237

people around. She ducked under the rope railing without anyone stopping her and ran to hide behind the nearest tent.

But moments later she shrank back as the tent flaps opened and a line of boys holding hymn books trooped out of it, wearing crisp, white choir robes with frilly white collars up to their ears. They were led by a master, holding a hand to his flapping, thick grey hair.

'Come along!' he called in a bossy voice. 'File in quickly and lift your surplices clear of the mud! I don't have enough spares for all of you and will *not* have you make me a laughing stock.'

The boys followed their master through an arched wooden door in the side of the Abbey, which swung shut with a bang behind them.

'I have an idea!' Penny whispered to the others. 'Just like Volantino, all we need to do is create a distraction.' She peeled back the canvas door and peeped inside. The marquee was empty, except for several benches and a litter of sandwich wrappers and paper cups that she guessed the choirboys had left behind. Penny darted her eyes over the debris, and then spotted what she was hoping to find: a heap of white fabric, lying on a bench. Resting her satchel down gently, she shook out a long, white garment, pushed her arms through the sleeves and yanked it over her coat. It sported several stains but was just the right size to cover up her normal clothes, and the high, frilly collar hid most of her bobbed hair. She dipped her hand in one of the paper cups and slicked her hair back with water, for good measure. 'What do you think?' she said.

'*Magnifique!*' exclaimed Bonvoyage, clapping his paws.

Wishyouwas tilted his head. 'You look like a he now,' he said with a quizzical frown.

Cartolina's eyes gleamed. 'Good idea, *Cara Penny!*'

Penny grinned. 'It was Volantino who gave me the idea. I can try and sneak into the Abbey in disguise. If I'm caught, Wishyouwas and Bonvoyage can use me as a distraction to run inside with the letter. Cartolina, will you be all right here with Volantino until we get back?'

'*Si!* We will rest here,' she said with a smile. 'The Secret Society is truly lucky to have you as members. Good luck and parcel's speed!'

Penny took a deep breath to steady her nerves. 'Let's go!' she said.

If anybody had been watching, they would have sworn they saw a late choirboy sprinting out of the marquee and along the stone wall of the Abbey, but all faces were fixed towards the entrance as the golden coach drew up.

Penny reached the door she had seen the choir enter yesterday. She twisted the ringbolt and for a horrible moment thought it might be locked, but then the door creaked open on to a dim stone passageway with a narrow staircase winding upwards. She quickly closed the door behind her, then leaned against it. 'We made it!' she panted. She heard Wishyouwas and Bonvoyage drop softly to the floor, but before they had taken a single step forward, a man in black robes with grey hair flapping up and down on his head hurried down the staircase. Penny froze. There was no time to run out again and the Sorters dived beneath her robe for cover. She stood fixed to the floor as the man halted, his face a shadowy mask. 'What are you doing here?' he demanded. 'The coronation is about to begin at any moment!'

Penny's heart fluttered as she tried to think. 'Sorry. I … um, needed the toilet?'

'That excuse might have worked for rehearsals, but not now,' thundered the man, who she guessed was the choirmaster. 'Come along, boy. Find your place at once. Up the stairs, go on!' He waved her onwards. Penny could hardly believe her narrow escape.

But then, just as she was passing him, the master clutched her sleeve and frowned, leaning closer. 'Hang on one moment,' he said. 'The toilet isn't in that direction. You don't look familiar either. Who are – Aargh!' He let go and started doing a jiggly dance. Penny saw a round lump running up and down his black sleeve and stifled a surprised giggle.

'Ha-help! Where'd it go?' the man cried, patting his body all over.

A small, furry head poked out from beneath his grey toupee. 'Run, you two!' hissed Bonvoyage, waving his paws frantically at the staircase. '*Vite!*'

Penny bolted, taking the stairs two at a time, the long choir robe almost tripping her. Wishyouwas leaped along beside her. A door at the top barred their way, but Penny tugged the handle and it swung open on to a high gallery. She turned and stumbled to a stop, her breath whooshing out of her.

For a moment she forgot everything except the colossal beauty of the scene before her. The gallery overlooked the Abbey, where thousands of beauti-fully dressed people sat either side of a wide, blue-carpeted aisle. They faced the royal throne, which was illuminated by rainbow-tinted daylight that slanted through the stained-glass rosette window. Resting upon a table behind it lay a sceptre, orb and crown, winking with rubies, sapphires and diamonds. There was a glowing, expectant magic in the air that made Penny shiver. Wishyouwas clambered up on to her shoulder, and his fur stood on end, prickling her cheek with electricity.

Penny tore her gaze away and searched for somewhere they could hide and wait for a chance to deliver the letter, but there were so many people. Immediately below them, the choirboys were sitting in rows, holding hymn sheets. A couple of them were turned towards her, nudging each other, and she blushed. Her heart and mind raced. Then she jumped as trumpets blasted a fanfare and the boys jerked their heads round and stood as one. The sonorous notes of an organ began to play a solemn, stirring anthem and their high, melodic voices soared into the vaulted roof.

Suddenly the entire congregation rose to its feet. The Queen, wearing a shimmering white silk gown, entered the Abbey and moved slowly along the aisle, followed by six ladies-in-waiting who held up her long, floating train. *Almost like a bride*, Penny thought, breathless at how magnificent she looked. 'Wishyouwas,' she whispered. 'I can't go any further, but you can. Now's the best time, while nobody's looking.' She nodded towards the throne.

'I – I isn't sure I can, Dear Penny,' Wishyouwas stammered, clutching his medallion.

'I know you can do it,' Penny said. 'You're a Deliverer, First Class.' She hugged him against her cheek. 'I believe in you.'

Wishyouwas swelled his small body with air. His face set in a determined frown, and he squared his tiny shoulders. Then, after a quick clasp of her neck, he dropped to the ground. Penny swallowed. From where she stood on the gallery, she was able to follow his path, down past the rows of choirboys, to a wooden railing. Then he vanished over the edge. Seconds later she caught a quick movement as he darted behind the cape of a watching duke. Wishyouwas paused there, his tail swishing side to side.

What's he doing? Penny wondered, her heart skittering in her chest. She'd imagined Wishyouwas would scurry towards the throne, but instead he hovered, looking as if he were getting ready to leap.

Just then the Queen walked past him. The long, flowing train of her dress followed, floating just above the ground like a flying carpet.

There was the fastest flash of brown – so quick Penny almost missed it – and Wishyouwas darted beneath the Queen's train. The tiniest of lumps bobbed along beneath the fabric, unnoticeable if you didn't know where to look.

It was such a daring, mad thing to do that a giggle exploded from Penny's mouth, an instant before a hand grabbed her by the shoulder. Her laughter was choked off as she was spun round.

'This is the boy ... I mean, *girl!*' said the choir-master, gaping at her with a blotchy, purplish face filled with rage. His hair had flopped to one side of his sweating, bald head and Penny realised it was a toupee. A guard with bushy eyebrows, the same one who had asked her for a pass yesterday, stood beside him with a fierce scowl.

Penny gulped, knowing she was in deep, deep trouble.

Wild Goose Chase

20

Wild Goose Chase

Penny was marched out of the gallery, through the dimly lit passageway and down the staircase. She looked everywhere for Bonvoyage, hoping he hadn't been caught or hurt, but there was no sign of him. She was let out of the Abbey and the lovely music and singing muffled to a faraway hum as the door closed. The choirmaster and guard stood before her, preventing her from running off.

'Explain *exactly* who you are and what you were doing sneaking inside Westminster Abbey pretending to be part of my choir!' hissed the master, whose toupee was now on back to front. Penny looked down at the ground, still searching for Bonvoyage. The wind whipped her hair out of her collar.

'You may well hang your head in shame!' snapped the choirmaster. 'Your behaviour is scandalous!'

'Hold on, I recognise you,' said the guard, peering closer. 'It's Penny Black, isn't it? You were here yesterday with Lady Vellum. I'm sorry,' he said more kindly, 'but the Royal Secretary won't be able to save you this time. She's inside the Abbey.'

Penny jerked her head up. 'No!' she cried. 'You have to get her out of there!'

The guard's gaze hardened again. 'Young lady,' he said in a low, warning tone. 'I do not think you know your place. I am not going to order ladies-in-waiting out of the Abbey while Her Majesty is being crowned, just to save you from getting into trouble.'

Penny's chest squeezed with panic. *I was so dazzled by the Queen, I didn't notice Lady Vellum was there!* she thought, silently kicking herself. Now Wishyouwas was right in her path. If he tried to deliver the letter, Lady Vellum would swoop on him.

'Indeed you do not know your place!' said the choirmaster. 'Silly girls like you should not expect to—'

'Penny!' yelled a distant but instantly familiar voice. 'Ma wee girl, there you are!'

Penny peered around the choirmaster and her heart almost burst. Her mother sprinted towards her from between the tents. The Court Postmaster, Mr Quilling, puffed like an engine just behind her. Uncle Frank hobbled as fast as he could on his stick at the back, with Hermes bounding along beside him. And, just visible against the greyhound's grey fur, Bonvoyage was riding on his back!

'Mum!' Penny cried, and tried to run forward, but both the choirmaster and the guard clamped her shoulders, pinning her to the spot.

Her mother's face changed instantly from tearful relief to outrage. 'Get away from ma daughter!' she shouted, her ginger hair tangled and wild in the wind. She reached Penny, pulled her away and stood in front of her, panting and furious. 'Get oota ma sight this very minute before I call the police!' she snarled, stamping her foot, and the two men backed away a step, their eyes wide.

'Excuse me, madam,' said the guard. 'But your daughter was caught trespassing inside the Abbey.'

Penny's mother swung round and stared. 'Is this true, Penny?' she said.

'Yes,' she said. 'We did go in, but—'

'We!' blurted the guard. 'What do you mean, "we"?'

'Me and … my friend,' Penny said.

'There's another one in there?' the choirmaster practically squeaked.

'Thank you – gentlemen – but – I have – this under – control. You – can go,' puffed Mr Quilling. He fished a rather crumpled yellow pass from his jacket pocket and handed it to the guard, who stood up straighter at once.

'Court Postmaster,' he said with a nod, and marched away.

'Well, if you're happy to take responsibility for this girl and her friend, that is fine by me!' said the choirmaster, adjusting his toupee before escaping inside the Abbey. Music and singing wafted out of the door, before going quiet again as it swung shut.

After that everyone stared at Penny with a mixture of shock, disbelief and, in Mr Quilling's case, extreme anger on their faces. Uncle Frank had reached them by now, and Bonvoyage jumped off Hermes and somersaulted on to the ground, before bowing to Penny with a flourish. '*Voilà!*' he said. 'I found – 'ow you say? – reinforcements?'

Penny's mother pulled her into a tight hug. 'I'm so happy you're safe.'

But Uncle Frank's eyebrows were arched like two archery bows. 'I think you owe us all an explanation,' he said. 'When your mother received your Mayday message we thought something terrible had happened to you.'

'We rushed straight to the palace, only to discover you had escaped!' her mother said. 'After being held in the guardroom with a nice lady called Spam, who explained all about the missing letter, Mr Quilling came and we tried to find you.'

Uncle Frank ruffled Hermes' head. 'Hermes tracked you through the park and along the river to the Abbey. Then your friend found us,' he said, nodding to Bonvoyage. 'What are you doing here, and dressed like that?'

Penny tried to speak, but something popped inside her. The tiredness and worry and fear of the past few hours came out in a sudden torrent. 'I'm sorry!' she said with a choke. 'But we had to escape from Lady Vellum. Then her falcon took the Monarch's Seal.'

Mr Quilling jerked. 'Lady Vellum, the Royal Secretary?'

The rest came out in a rush as Penny told them about the trail of fake clues and how they had discovered Lady Vellum was the real thief behind the missing Monarch's Seal. Mr Quilling's eyes grew wider and wider. 'But Wishyouwas managed to rescue the letter from her falcon. I sneaked into the Abbey and he's still in there, trying to deliver it to the Queen. But Lady Vellum's in there too!'

Mr Quilling's moustache quivered. He stared at Penny, and she could see a whirlwind of thoughts racing in his eyes. He blinked, checked his watch, blinked again, and then to her astonishment held out his hand. 'We'll need to work together to stop her before it's too late.'

'Then you believe me?' Penny said, feeling strangely as if she liked him. Only hours ago he had been ordering the Bureau to be torn apart. Now, she felt hope.

Mr Quilling's mouth and moustache became a grim line. 'I've wanted to believe you all along,' he said. 'I had a suspicion about Lady Vellum being something other than she seemed, but I didn't have a scrap of proof – until now. She has led us all on a wild goose chase.'

Penny felt as if a sack of letters had been lifted off her shoulders.

'Follow me,' said Mr Quilling.

'Wait,' said Penny, and she ran to fetch Cartolina and Volantino from the tent. Uncle Frank carried them in her satchel as she hurried behind the Court Postmaster.

He thumped up to the Abbey entrance and spoke to the same guard who had caught Penny. The soldier stood straight, nodded and led them inside, through a maze of old stone corridors.

Finally, they reached a low wooden door deep inside the Abbey, and halted.

Mr Quilling checked his watch again and whispered. 'By my reckoning she should be in there now, getting ready for the crowning ceremony. Just you,' he said to Penny. 'The rest of you, come with me quickly to the other side.'

'Who is in there?' Penny asked, but Mr Quilling had already left.

'Good luck, Pen!' Uncle Frank said, giving her a thumbs up.

Penny swallowed her nerves, and went in.

21

One More Twist

Penny edged through the door, into a small
octagonal chamber. Then she froze. The
Queen herself was standing right in front of her,
being helped by her ladies-in-waiting to remove
the long train from her dress. They crouched on
the ground, and she couldn't see where Lady
Vellum was, or if Wishyouwas was there either.
'Y-Your Majesty!' she stammered, remembering to
curtsy.

'Penny Black!' replied the Queen with a warm
smile, as if it were not at all strange to see a girl

wearing a choir robe pop out of nowhere during the middle of her coronation. 'To what do I owe this unexpected pleasure?'

At the same time Lady Vellum's head jerked up from where she had been unpinning the train, and her eyes became two poison darts. She crushed the fabric in her fists.

'Um,' Penny said. 'I – I mean, we …'

The Queen turned. 'Ladies, would you mind allowing us a few moments of privacy?' The ladies-in-waiting curtsied and left the room, all except for Lady Vellum, who hovered beside the Queen. 'Your Majesty, Penny Black and I are well acquainted, aren't we?' She beamed a wide, toothy smile at Penny. 'Where is your dear little friend, Wishyouwas? You two never go anywhere without the other.'

'I is here!' said a muffled squeak, and a lump wriggled from beneath the folds of fabric on the floor. Wishyouwas emerged, his fur sticking up.

The Queen's eyes twinkled as he bowed low, touching the floor with his nose. 'We is here to deliver your letter, Dear Royal Postmistress,' he said. He untied the canister strapped to his back and held it up to her in a slightly trembling paw.

'The Monarch's Seal?' the Queen asked, with a tone of slight surprise. 'How wonderful of the Sorters to deliver it. I am glad it has been in such safe paws.' Penny wrinkled her nose in confusion. Why hadn't she mentioned it being lost?

The Queen unscrewed the lid and pulled out a rolled-up envelope. Penny glanced at Lady Vellum and was startled to see a thin smile on her lips. Her throat tightened. Something was wrong …

The Queen unrolled the envelope, but there was no wax seal. She pulled it open and carefully removed a letter from inside. After taking the tiniest of breaths, she unfolded the paper.

'This letter appears to be written by Mr Quilling, the Court Postmaster,' she said, with a slight catch in her voice. 'It tells me that the Monarch's Seal is missing, presumed stolen?'

Penny opened her mouth but couldn't speak. Wishyouwas stiffened, his body like a small brown rock. 'I d-doesn't understand,' he stammered.

'I understand perfectly!' said Lady Vellum, and her grey eyes sparkled with an icy, triumphant gleam. 'I regret to inform Your Majesty that the Sorters stole this letter, as well as the Monarch's Seal! It was *I* who first suspected their misdeeds, after important mail began going missing from the palace. Fortunately Mr Quilling has wisely closed down the Bureau forever.'

Wishyouwas's fur darkened instantly. 'Sorters never steal!' he squeaked.

Penny managed to find her voice. 'Why would we deliver a stolen letter? The Sorters are innocent. The real thief is *you*!'

'Ha ha!' Lady Vellum laughed. It sounded like a hunting cry. 'How preposterous, accusing *me*, a lady, and Royal Secretary to boot! You see they will stop at nothing, Your Majesty. They are traitors and spies, every last one of them!'

The Queen calmly folded the letter, slid it

back inside the envelope and returned it with the canister to Wishyouwas. 'Is my father's letter truly lost?' she asked with a hint of sadness in her voice.

Penny felt a pang in her chest. 'Didn't you know, Your Majesty?' she asked.

'I was unaware it was missing, until now.'

Penny frowned. 'But your summons letter said—'

'What summons letter?' Lady Vellum interrupted, edging closer to Penny. 'Show us. Do you have it with you now?'

Penny's mouth was so dry she couldn't swallow. *I told Lady Vellum that I lost it in the wind!* The truth was all twisted, and she couldn't think of any way to untangle it. She looked at Wishyouwas. His paws hung limply against his sides, and his tail flopped against the floor. After everything they had been through, they had failed.

Lady Vellum coiled her silver fingernails around Penny's wrist like talons. 'Come with me, child,' she said in a hiss, leaning so close that Penny caught the flash of her silver chain around her neck. 'You have wasted quite enough of Her Majesty's time.'

Penny let out a gasp and jerked her arm out of Lady Vellum's grasp. 'I know where the real Monarch's Seal is hidden!' she cried.

Lady Vellum's pupils flared and she took a step back. 'So, at last you confess!' she said. 'This girl is in league with the Sorters, Your Majesty. No wonder they have managed to evade capture for so long. A child is a convenient cover for their crimes. Look at how she has already sneaked into the Abbey!'

'That is *quite* enough, Lady Vellum,' said the Queen, holding up her hand, and the Royal Secretary was forced to be quiet. Then she turned to Penny. 'Where do you believe the Monarch's Seal to be?' she asked.

Penny took a sharp breath. This was, after all, still only a guess. She glanced at Wishyouwas, who nodded back, his eyes wide and full of trust. 'It is hidden inside Lady Vellum's fountain pen,' she said.

Lady Vellum's hand flew to her neck, but she dropped it quickly. 'How ridiculous!' she snorted.

'You cannot believe a word this child or this creature says!'

'This *Sorter*,' corrected the Queen. 'Your pen, Lady Vellum, if you please,' she said, holding out her hand. 'I noticed you were wearing it while you were unpinning my train.'

Lady Vellum's smile flickered. 'But you shall get ink on your dress, Your Majesty,' she said. The Queen did not reply.

Lady Vellum's grey eyes began to flicker left and right. 'I am feeling rather faint,' she said, clasping her neck, which had turned red and blotchy. 'Perhaps some fresh air ...' There was a sudden *snap*. She yanked the chain off her neck with the fountain pen attached and threw it as far away from her as she could. It spun through the air and Lady Vellum fled towards a door on the other side of the chamber.

A brown ball leaped past Penny's nose. Wishyouwas whipped out his paw and snatched the pen in mid-air before landing on his paws. He darted back to Penny's side and passed it to her.

Lady Vellum reached the door and wrenched it open, only to find the way barred by Uncle Frank's walking stick, a furious Mr Quilling and an even more furious Mrs Black, accompanied by the guard. 'Let me out!' she screeched, attempting to barge past them.

'Royal Secretary,' said the Queen, in a soft and steady voice. 'You are relieved of your duties, with immediate effect.'

Lady Vellum spun round, glaring at Penny and Wishyouwas. 'You meddling rodents have undone everything!'

'You planned it all,' Penny said, and as the pieces began to fall into place in her mind, she felt suddenly confident and sure of herself. 'It was you stealing the letters from the palace, wasn't it? You were scared the Sorters would find out, so you hid the Monarch's Seal inside your pen just before it was put in the Red Box to be delivered. I bet you made sure the van stopped at the traffic lights too, so Mr Quilling would think the Sorters could have taken it. But you made a mistake.' She glanced at

Wishyouwas and smiled. 'Nothing is ever lost that cannot be solved.'

'I never make mistakes. My plan was perfect!' Lady Vellum raised her hands, clawing the air. Her eyes were hate-filled pinpricks. 'I stole the most valuable letter in the world. I will be remembered as the greatest spy there has ever been, and you will be destroyed!' She launched forward to attack.

Faster than a blink Wishyouwas leaped through the air, the leather cord from the canister in his paw. He landed on Lady Vellum's wrists and his fingers were a blur as he wrapped the cord around them. She snarled and struggled but he pulled tight and tied a complicated parcel knot.

'You gotted away with nothing. You has been sorted!' he squeaked.

'Come with me.' The guard took charge and led Lady Vellum away, kicking and thrashing in her silk skirts, but her threats soon faded.

Mr Quilling entered the room and dipped his head. 'Your Majesty, may I beg your forgiveness? I should have informed you in person of the missing

Monarch's Seal, instead of relying on letters and Lady Vellum's words. Perhaps this mess could have been avoided.'

'There is nothing to forgive. Lady Vellum hoodwinked us all, Court Postmaster,' said the Queen.

'Thank you, Your Majesty!' Mr Quilling said with a bow.

The Queen rested her gaze on Wishyouwas and Penny. 'As for sending important messages by letter, fortunately we have the most trusted guardians in the realm on our side.'

Penny felt herself lift to her toes, and Wishyouwas looked two inches taller.

'Now, perhaps it is time we opened the Monarch's Seal?'

'We'll give you all some privacy and wait outside,' Penny's mother said, and she and Uncle Frank left.

Penny passed the fountain pen back to Wishyouwas, but he shook his head.

'Let us deliver it together,' he squeaked.

He climbed on to her arm and Penny stepped up

to the Queen. Wishyouwas put his paw on her hand as she placed the pen in the Queen's palm. *What if we're wrong again?* she thought. They had already been tricked twice.

Penny gripped Wishyouwas's finger as the Queen unscrewed the top of the pen. She paused a moment, as if gathering her thoughts, and then gave it one more twist. She pulled a tightly rolled-up letter from inside. As she unrolled it, red powder drifted to the floor and a large, round wax seal appeared, laced all over with cracks. It fell to pieces as the Queen broke it to open the envelope. Then

she slid out the letter and began reading in the softest of murmurs:

'*Dear Lilibet. This letter is filled, not with top-secret information as another sort of person might expect, but with belief and love. You are ready for this next step, my daughter. You always have been ...*'

The Queen stopped reading and looked at them both, her eyes shining. 'Thank you so very much,' she said in a soft voice. 'You have brought me home.'

After that, everything became a great hurry. The ladies-in-waiting returned and they dressed the Queen in a long purple robe, ready for her crown-ing ceremony. Penny was taken by Mr Quilling to a seat *inside* the Abbey, between her mother and Uncle Frank. Bonvoyage, Cartolina and Volantino nestled in the satchel to watch, and Wishyouwas perched on Penny's lap.

'I didn't need to rent that television after all!' Uncle Frank said under his breath, and Penny stifled a happy laugh.

The glittering crown, orb and sceptre were bestowed upon the Queen, right in front of them.

Then the Abbey erupted with deafening cries of 'God save the Queen!'

Penny shivered from her hair down to her toes.

'Quite something, wasn't it?' said Mr Quilling after the Queen had departed the Abbey. He looked at Penny and Wishyouwas with a curious glint in his eyes. 'I'm bursting to ask. How did you know the letter was inside Lady Vellum's fountain pen?'

'She didn't sign my pass with it the first time we were here,' Penny said.

'So there wasn't never any ink in it,' added Wishyouwas.

'Well, well, so the real Monarch's Seal was hiding in plain sight all along,' said Mr Quilling with a shake of his head. He tugged his whiskery side-burns. 'It's no wonder Lady Vellum wanted the Sorters gone, what with brains and paws like yours. Ever since your existence became known last Christmas, she must have worried about her letter thefts and spying being discovered, and started plotting the Sorters' downfall. Perhaps there will be more mysteries the Sorters can help us with in the future.'

He stood up, and a serious expression crossed his face. 'For now, though, I have a lot of lost letters to return, and a *big* apology to make.'

22

Final Farewells

That afternoon Penny was so busy she almost forgot she was leaving London in just a few hours.

It took an enormous operation to put the Bureau back to rights. Mr Quilling, Spam and the rest of his staff from the palace arrived on the Special Branch, bringing with them sacks of confiscated lost letters, along with some mysterious extra hampers, baskets and boxes. After Mr Quilling had made a solemn apology to all the Sorters, he helped to pass letters from the sacks to their tiny paws. The Sorters, including Cartolina and Bonvoyage, formed a chain and whisked the letters away to be re-sorted. Penny and her mother stood by the Front Gate and helped carry in the heavier parcels. After a while Penny lost sight of Wishyouwas. Uncle Frank had also disappeared somewhere.

'Do you think they're all right?' Penny asked, scanning her eyes over the tunnel for any sign of them.

'They've both probably done enough delivering for one day,' her mother said, rubbing her back. 'And look, we're nearly finished!'

Sure enough, the last of the sacks was soon emptied. Mr Quilling thumped over and shook Penny's hand. 'I must return to the palace,' he said. 'I have an urgent telegram to send.' He glanced at Penny's mother and nodded. 'Spam will be staying. I – ah – think she deserves it too.'

'Deserves what?' Penny asked, but Mr Quilling was already thumping away. She jumped as Wishyouwas bounced on to her shoulder out of nowhere. 'Where have you been?' she said with a grin.

'With me!' Uncle Frank answered. He tapped up to them on his walking stick, and leaned against it. He coughed and cleared his throat. 'I'm – ah – sorry you two didn't have a leaving party at the post office as planned.'

A painful ache grew in Penny's chest. 'That doesn't matter,' she said.

'Yes it does,' Wishyouwas squeaked. 'Come on!' He tugged Penny by her hair towards the opposite end of the tunnel so insistently that she laughed. Then from up ahead she heard a bell tinkle, and the Sorters stopped what they were doing and raced on all fours alongside her.

When they eventually rounded the corner to the letterbox avenue, Penny stopped and caught her breath in wonder.

'We does this for you, Dear Penny,' Wishyouwas said.

The avenue had been totally transformed, looking like a splendid, multicoloured wonderland.

Twinkling fairy lights were looped between the letterboxes, which had their doors wide open. The ground in front of them had been laid with newspaper, and basket hampers made tables. Best of all, dozens of paper plates contained a feast fit for the Queen! There were savouries of all sorts, sandwiches and scones, jams and marmalades of every imaginable flavour, clotted cream and whipped cream and even *real* ice cream inside a metal box filled with ice cubes! Now Penny realised what was in all those extra boxes Mr Quilling had brought.

'For *me*?' she said, swallowing a lump in her throat.

Wishyouwas nodded, and his toes curled on her shoulder. 'We wanted to say a proper goodbye.'

Uncle Frank laid a hand gently on her other shoulder. 'Mr Quilling was more than happy to help with our *under*-the-street party,' he said with a chuckle.

Four human-sized cushions were set in pride of place beside Their Highnesses' postbox. Dearsir and Dearmadam sat on their inkwell thrones, smiling down at the gathering Sorters, who clustered all around the edges, their eyes bulging at the feast. Then Stampduty thumped his yellow pencil. But instead of demanding silence, he called: 'All be seated. Let there be music!' The lovely song 'I Believe' floated gently along the tunnel from a borrowed gramophone. The spell broke, and the tunnel filled with high, excited twittering, munching and crunching, slurping and burping as the Sorters fell on the feast. Penny nestled on to a cushion between her uncle and Spam, who were talking non-stop. Wishyouwas waved his paws in the air as he told wide-eyed Withlove about their adventures. Penny bit into a mouth-watering slice of pear tart, but her heart felt almost too full to eat.

'*Voilà!*' Bonvoyage's muffled voice came from behind a plate piled so high with cheese and crackers, sponge cake, meringues and slices of pie that Penny couldn't see him. He set it down, knocking several crackers to the floor, then swept off his cap, revealing a large chunk of cheddar cheese, which he bit into.

Cartolina carried over a much more modest plate of food and sat next to Penny's foot. Volantino waddled beside her and pecked happily at a fallen cracker.

'So, Bonvoyage, do you still think the British Sorters are nincompoops who live in a smelly underground cave, as you put it?' Cartolina said.

Bonvoyage almost choked and spat out the cheese. 'Who said this? *Moi?* No, never 'ave I said such a terrible thing! *Le Bureau est très beau.* Very beautiful.' Suddenly he let out a loud sniff and dabbed his eyes with his cap, turning it soggy. 'I will post you many letters from France, *mes amis.*'

Cartolina's eyes glistened as she too looked from Wishyouwas to Penny. 'Remember, we will always be a society,' she said. 'Our help is only a letter away.'

Penny smiled and nodded. But the ache in her chest grew heavier. She would miss them terribly after they left for France and Italy by sea and air. It seemed the rest of the Sorters would too. Between them, they now had at least a dozen new pen pals. The Secret Society of Very Important Post was stronger than ever before.

Her mum chatted in French with Bonvoyage, while Cartolina showed Withlove how to swirl her ruler in the air like a baton. Volantino waddled around them, pecking so many crumbs that Penny doubted if he would be able to fly the next day. She couldn't help glancing at her pendant and the paperclip ticking past the hours and minutes, far faster than normal, it seemed. Very soon it would be time to leave. She fell quiet, and Wishyouwas also seemed lost in his own thoughts.

Bonvoyage finally lay back against her cushion, patting his swollen tummy, which looked as if he'd swallowed an orange whole.

Cartolina rolled her eyes at him and dabbed her whiskers with her handkerchief cape, then let out a hiccup. '*Mi scusi!*' she said, blushing.

A bell rang. The Sorters sat as straight as they could manage and turned towards the postbox as Dearsir and Dearmadam heaved to their paws.

'We wish to make an announcement,' trilled Dearmadam. 'Since the Special Branch that connects our Bureau to Buckingham Palace is now an open secret among us, and following the seriousness of the missing Monarch's Seal, we believe it is essential that a special department of Sorters is formed to ensure any lost letters for Her Royal Postmistress are safely delivered.'

Ears everywhere perked up and the Sorters murmured to themselves, their excited whispers blowing like a soft breeze through the tunnel.

'The new Special Branch department requires a leader,' croaked Dearsir. Before he had even finished speaking, two paws shot into the air, halfway down the avenue.

Private and Confidential stood on their tiptoes, so tall they looked about to take flight.

'Your Highnesses! Might SWALK make a humble recommendation as to who among us is most fit to lead this department?' enquired Private.

Penny groaned inwardly. Bonvoyage leaped to

his paws, clearly ready to argue with them, but Cartolina tugged his tail to make him sit down again.

Dearsir and Dearmadam inclined their heads.

The two Solvers suddenly swivelled on their paws and pointed straight towards where Penny was sitting. Her heart began to thrum – no, not towards *her*, towards …

'We recommend Wishyouwas!' said Confidential. 'We can think of no Sorter who is more trusted and capable.'

'He truly *is* a First Class Deliverer,' added Private. 'The very best the Bureau has.'

Wishyouwas's whole body swelled. He held his breath, turning a funny shade of brown, while Stampduty thumped his pencil for a vote. 'All in favour of Wishyouwas becoming the new Special Branch leader, raise your paws,' he called.

Hundreds of paws flew upwards and the air erupted with cheers, loudest of all from Penny. Volantino flapped over their heads, cooing his approval. The sound echoed through the tunnels, going on and on for what felt like forever.

Wishyouwas finally let his breath out in one long gust. He smiled at Penny, and his fur seemed to be glowing from the inside out.

23

A New Home

That night, Penny stood beside her mother beneath the arches of Euston Station, chewing her fingernails. Neither of them spoke much. The platform teemed with other people laughing and hugging and waving farewell to friends and relatives, their faces alight with excitement before clambering aboard the chugging steam train.

Penny scanned the ground, looking for the tell-tale flicker of paws or brown fur. 'I thought he might come to say goodbye,' she said, then checked the time for the hundredth occasion on her Sorters' pendant.

'Oh, Penny,' said her mum. 'I'm sure he would have come if he could. Wishyouwas must be rushed off his paws with his new job at the Bureau. Is there something you wanted to say?'

'Not really, it's just ...' Penny was interrupted by an announcement over the station tannoy and her heart sank further:

'*This is the final call for the ten o'clock Caledonian Sleeper to Aberdeen, departing on Platform Three in five minutes.*'

'Well, I suppose we should find our cabin,' said her mother. She picked up their overnight bags and turned towards the train.

And then, as if Wishyouwas had whispered into her ear, Penny knew that there *was* something she couldn't leave London without saying after all. She reached forward and tugged her mother's coat sleeve. 'Mum,' she said. 'There's something I want to tell you. Only, you might get upset, and ...' She trailed off and a tear slid down her nose and plopped on to the platform concrete.

Her mother put down the bags and rested both hands upon Penny's shoulders. 'What is it, love?' she asked. 'You can tell me.'

Penny raised her face. 'I – I want us to spend more time together more than anything. But I'm really going to miss Uncle Frank and Wishyouwas and all the Sorters, here in London.'

Saying it instantly made her feel better, but then her mother let out a deep sigh, and for a horrible moment Penny worried she had badly hurt her feelings. Then she said, 'Me too, Penny. I feel the same way.'

Penny wiped her eyes on her sleeve. 'You do, really?'

Her mother nodded. 'Flying was keeping me away from you, just when you needed me the most,' she said. 'I want that to change. But … I *am* going to miss being a pilot. It makes me sad to think about it, but I didn't want to upset you by saying so.'

'It doesn't,' said Penny. 'I'm glad you told me.'

'Do you think we will be all right?' her mother asked.

'I know we will,' Penny said, smiling.

They folded into each other's arms and stayed like that, wrapped together, until Penny felt a tap upon her shoulder.

'Ahem – sorry for interrupting,' said someone in a familiar, breathless Welsh accent. 'But I wonder if I might speak with you both?'

Penny spun round. 'Mr Quilling!' she exclaimed.

The Court Postmaster, as walrus-like as ever with his bristly whiskers, was sweating as if he'd run a mile. 'I wanted to catch you,' he panted. 'What I wanted to ask – if you don't mind, of course – is …'

The train whistle blew, drowning his last words.

'I am so sorry, Mr Quilling,' said Penny's mum. 'But we really must be going now.'

'That's exactly what I'm here to stop you doing,' gasped Mr Quilling.

'Stop us! Why?' asked Penny's mother. 'There isn't anything else wrong, is there?'

'No, no,' said Mr Quilling. He seemed nervous and totally unlike the gruff, unfriendly man Penny had first met. 'Only, I hoped you might come and work for me instead.'

'Oh!' Penny's mother said. 'I am sorry to disappoint you, but I already have a job, in Aberdeen. And if we miss this train, I will almost certainly lose it.'

'Do not worry about that, the postmaster there is a pen pal of mine,' said Mr Quilling. 'I've already sent him a telegram, in the hope you might say yes, and he gave his blessing, if you do. Anyhow, I might have lost *my* job, if it wasn't for Penny and the Sorters,' he said. 'You see, it's my duty to safely deliver letters on behalf of Her Majesty. That includes flying post abroad. If you come and work for me, you can fly as little or often as you like and help me at the Court Post Office in between. How does that sound?'

Penny and her mother both caught their breaths at the same moment.

'You mean we can still stay in London?' Penny said.

'And I can still be a pilot?' asked her mother.

Mr Quilling nodded. His face was turning red, as if he were holding his breath.

'W-well, I …' Penny's mother stuttered. 'It's a very kind offer. Penny, what do you think?'

Penny was already jumping up and down. 'I think it's perfect!' she said.

'Stupendous!' Mr Quilling's breath rushed out of him. His moustache lifted like an extra smile. 'Come with me, I've got a post van being guarded outside. We'll drive you to your address.'

'Oh, um …' Penny's mother's cheeks turned postbox red. 'We don't have an address in London any more,' she said. 'We left our old home and all of our belongings are now in Aberdeen, you see …'

'But of course you have an address here!' interrupted Mr Quilling, his eyes twinkling. 'The job comes with accommodation too. Didn't I mention that?'

Penny and her mother glanced at each other. 'Where?' they asked at the same time.

'Why, you'll be living at the palace, of course,' he said.

Penny gaped at him. 'You don't mean *Buckingham Palace*?'

The Court Postmaster nodded. 'The Queen requested it herself. The suite of rooms used to belong to a certain ex-Royal Secretary, and very nice they are too, overlooking the gardens. Might want a bit of a colour change though. And as for your belongings, you can fly to Scotland as soon as you like and collect them. Take it as a holiday and see a bit of the country, if you wish.'

'I don't believe it,' said Penny's mother, blinking as if she had just woken up. 'I simply don't believe it.'

Feeling as if she had sprouted wings, Penny practically floated through the station. She didn't even notice the train whistle blowing before it chugged away without them. *If only Wishyouwas were here, so I could tell him!* she thought. She made up her mind to write to him at the Bureau as soon as they arrived.

Parked on a quiet road outside was a Royal Mail van. As soon as Mr Quilling opened the passenger door, something small, brown and furry flew at Penny and landed on her shoulder. Two warm, velvety paws clasped her neck.

'Wishyouwas!' she cried, and whirled him around with joy. 'Have you heard the news?'

He nodded. 'Now you is able to come to the burrow whenever you want on the Special Branch, Dear Penny!' he squeaked.

'Yes, it's all worked out very nicely in the end,' agreed Mr Quilling a few minutes later, as he drove them along the London streets. 'Though I must admit, for a moment there at the Abbey, I thought we had lost the Monarch's Seal forever!'

Just then they reached Birdcage Walk, and the white pillars of Buckingham Palace became visible at the end of the long road. Although it was late, the pavements lining St James's Park were still crowded with people, and for some reason they were all looking up, craning their necks towards the night sky. Penny and Wishyouwas pressed their noses to the van's window and stared upwards together …

They jumped as, with a thunderous *boom*, the sky exploded with fireworks, lighting up the palace with a million brilliant, multicoloured stars.

Almost, Penny thought happily, as if they were guiding her home.

Author's Note

I finished writing this story just as Queen Elizabeth's reign ended, almost seventy years since her coronation on 2nd June 1953. It has been a great privilege to bring that historic day to life on these pages. The Sorter's version may differ somewhat from the official history books but, after all, almost nobody knew they were present while the Queen was being crowned.

If you ever visit London and decide to follow the Sorters' trail, take a stroll along Birdcage Walk and turn into St James's Park. There, nestled beside the bank of a canal, you will find a pretty, gingerbread-style cottage. Duck Island Cottage was once the home of birdkeeper Thomas Hinton, until he retired in early 1953. For over fifty years Tom protected the waterfowl of the park and rescued many other birds, including a famous African sea-eagle called

'Portugese Jack' who escaped from London Zoo. After Tom left, Duck Island Cottage was abandoned for many years. Happily, it was saved from being demolished and is now the headquarters of London Historic Parks and Gardens Trust. On the way there, perhaps stop at the Boy Statue fountain and catch a glimpse of Buckingham Palace between the trees. Like Penny and Wishyouwas, who knows what else you might discover?

About the Author

Alexandra Page spent her early childhood being airmailed between England and Zimbabwe and making up stories to entertain her younger siblings. After studying English Literature at University College London, she worked for several years in book production and then in the City, before venturing into writing. *Wishyouwas* was Alexandra's first children's book. It won the WriteMentor Children's Novel Award in 2019 and was shortlisted for the Times/Chicken House Children's Fiction Competition and the CrimeFest Award for Best Crime Novel for Children. Alexandra loves being creative, travelling to far-flung places and swimming in anything bigger than a puddle. She lives in London with her husband and daughter.

About the Illustrator

Penny Neville-Lee was raised on a healthy diet of Saturday cartoons and MGM musicals. Never happier than when creating, she spent her early years drawing and making, and was rarely found without a doodle somewhere in the margins. Penny studied for a Painting MA at the Royal College of Art. After several years making large oil paintings of gloomy woods in the company of Radio 4 and some studio mice, she had her small son, shifted to the kitchen table and realised there might be something in those doodles after all. Penny is inspired by small people, bright colours, a blank page and newly sharpened pencils. She lives in Manchester with her two children, husband and very adventurous cat.